REPOE MAN

PAMELA COWAN

COPYRIGHT

REPOE MAN

ISBN-13: 978-1-957638-96-6 (Print)
ISBN-13: 978-1-957638-97-3 (eBook)
First Edition – Printed in the United States

818 SW 3rd Avenue, #221-2218
Portland, OR 97204-2405
855-649-0821

DEDICATION AND ACKNOWLEDGMENT

This book is dedicated to the original, and real, Bobby Poe and to our mutual friend and author, Jake Elliot. Not only did you both inspire this book and help with some of its content (the good stuff), but you also hung out online with me during the incredibly dull days of early Covid. Hey, we shared living through a plague, is there really anything more to say?

For insight into Bobby's time in the military, as well as nefarious limo companies, I'd like to thank Army Veteran, J.R. Rolandson.

Thank you also, as always, to Jim, Jason and Jeanne for your unfailing patience and support.

OTHER TITLES BY THIS AUTHOR

Storm McKenzie Vigilante Series

Storm Justice

Storm Vengeance

Storm Retribution

Eulalona County Thrillers

Something in The Dark (Mystery)

Cold Kill (Suspense)

The EL & Em Detective Series

Fire and Lies
Hide and Sneak

Fantasy and Science Fiction

Yetzirah

Altered Visions

REPOE MAN

PAMELA COWAN

CHAPTER ONE

I got released from jail at the ungodly hour of four thirty in the morning. They said it had something to do with waiting for paperwork. I thought it had more to do with not wanting newly released prisoners mingling with law-respecting citizens.

Whatever the reason I didn't care. I was just glad to be out. The sky was dark but streetlights and the ring of lights around the perimeter of the jail's fenced yard were blazing. All that light turned the teeth of the razor wire white, like sharks' teeth.

It looked strange. Everything did. The moment was full of contrasts. I was tired but also wired. I was bummed I'd had to ask Jake to pick me up but happy he was going to be there. It had been a long time since I'd seen him. I'd spent a full year inside.

"Was it worth it?" one of the jailers asked, as he handed me a plastic bag with my stuff. The bag had my name written neatly in black Sharpie by someone who'd obviously practiced their letters in kindergarten. POE, ROBERT. I took the bag, thinking how it, and a six-by-eight storage locker, held all my worldly possessions. I'd never had much, but this was pathetic.

I put the thirty-seven dollars in my wallet and then slid the wallet into the back pocket of my jeans. Eighteen cents, a set of keys, and two braided leather bracelets, gifts from an ex-girlfriend, went into a jacket pocket. No phone. It had been broken in the fight that landed me here. As I was taking my stuff out of the bag and putting it away, I thought about his question. Was it worth it?

The day had started okay. I'd been on my bike, heading north up 101 from Los Angelas. Since I'd be going through her town, I thought I might as well swing by and see Zoey. A lame reason, I know. The truth was I wanted to see her and would have driven thousands of miles to make that happen. Jake, Zoey, and I had sort of grown up together. Anyway, we'd spent several years in the same foster home. Jake was like a brother but—right or wrong--Zoey was never like a sister.

I hadn't seen her in nearly three years, but I knew if I called Jake, he would have her address. For some reason, he'd made it his mission to keep in touch with all the kids who lived with us in foster care, no matter for how long. Sure enough, he had it.

When I got to her place I was impressed. It was nice. Not an LA mansion but seriously nice, with a big yard, what the fancy folk call grounds, and a wrought iron gate at the end of the driveway. The gate was open, so I drove right up to the house, got off the bike, and knocked on the door. Zoey answered. I was kind of expecting a maid or something, so I was a little surprised.

I remember it so clearly. The big oak door swung open and there she stood, all that long blond hair, those big brown eyes, and that heart-shaped face. Zoey. She put her hand over her mouth, kind of a nervous gesture and I noticed her hand was shaking.

She seemed anxious, scared even, and that was strange. It was just me. Then someone deep in the house barked something and Zoey flinched. I looked closer and saw she was wearing a ton of makeup. When I realized what that makeup was probably covering, when I thought of that flinch, a primal rage swept through me.

Pushing past her, I marched down the hall, my boots pounding on the floor as if I were trying to slam my foot through the polished marble tiles with each step. I had tunnel vision, the edges of that hallway were black, and all my senses fixated on a narrow target, a man's voice.

I found him sitting on a big white couch in a huge living room, paperwork spread around him on the floor, the coffee table. He was big and blond and a little too good-looking. The kind of guy you see and think, professional tennis coach, amateur slimeball. Or maybe that's just my own personal prejudice. I didn't slow, just reached down, got a handful of his shirt, and pulled him up so I could hit him. It felt good. Every time I hit him it felt good.

"Yeah," I told the jailer. "Yeah, it was worth it." I

tossed the plastic bag in the trash, pushed open the door, and stepped outside.

I had been waiting for no more than ten minutes when a car drove up. A vintage Chevy Malibu with gray-green custom paint, almost black under the lights. Jake hit the horn. When I got close, he reached over and popped the door. I slipped in and sank deep into the heated seat. That wasn't stock. Neither was the smell of fresh leather, but I appreciated it anyway.

"1970?" I asked.

Jake smiled and revved the engine.

"454?" I asked.

He nodded. "You know it."

"Son of a bitch. You know this is one of my dream cars."

"Yeah, I know. What can I tell you, Bobby, you always had good taste."

I fumbled around and pulled on my seat belt. "Thanks for picking me up."

Jake shrugged. "No problem. Anywhere you want to go?"

"Food?" I asked. All I'd been thinking about for

two days was a hamburger and not just any hamburger. The jail served hamburgers, flat grayish pucks of something they called meat, served on a stale bun with limp lettuce.

"What kind of food?" Jake asked.

"I don't know, maybe a pepper bacon burger from Burgerville with some cheese, red onions, tomato, lettuce, extra pickle, on a sesame seed bun."

"Haven't given this much thought, have you."

"And a shake. Oh, and fries. Family-sized potato fries, not that weird sweet potato crap."

"Fine, we'll find one on the way."

Half an hour later a sign on the side of the highway welcomed us to Oregon. I put my head back and closed my eyes. The next time I opened them was when the car bounced over a speed bump, and we were pulling into a Burgerville.

We went inside. At that early hour, the restaurant was nearly empty. One young guy with a pile of books sat in a corner sipping a soda. His leather backpack was on the floor, one strap wrapped around his ankle as if he feared its imminent departure. We got our food, a pile of stuff for me, fries, and free water for Jake, and took a table as far from the college kid as we could get.

"Could have had some of my fries," I said, nodding toward the huge pile in front of me.

"And risk losing a hand. No thanks. So, was it worth it?" Jake asked me.

"You too? That's what the guy who just let me out asked me, and yes, of course it was."

"Because it was Zoey?"

"Because the guy was a dick. I'm over Zoey."

Jake made a snorting noise.

I ignored him and took a drink of the chocolate shake. I didn't know what was better, the taste or the sugar rush. I *was* over her, damnit. I just forgot for a minute. The minute I saw her.

"You told me you knocked him around a little."

"Yeah."

"Zoey said it was a little more than that."

"When did you talk to Zoey?"

"Yesterday. She heard you were getting out, so she called. Wants me to let her know if you're okay."

I took another drink of my shake to show I was being nonchalant. "She around?"

"No, she got a big payoff in the divorce and took off for somewhere less wet and lots warmer. Mexico, I think, but she wasn't real forthcoming.

Yesterday was the first time I'd heard from her in nearly a year. She was rattled after the fight. Told me she couldn't make you stop. You put him in the hospital with a broken arm, broken ribs, busted jaw, a serious concussion, and some other miscellaneous cuts and bruises."

"Yeah, well he shouldn't have touched her."

"True."

"Lucky I didn't kill him."

Jake nodded. "The lawyer told Zoey her bruises got you charged with a misdemeanor instead of a felony assault, so one year in jail versus five in prison. That was lucky too."

I took a huge bite of the hamburger, partly because I was starving, and the smell was making my mouth water. Partly to get Jake to stop talking.

It worked, and for a while, there was nothing but the steady hum of a fan somewhere and the sound of me grinding happily through a couple of thousand calories.

After we finished and got back into Jake's car, he reached out and punched a button on the dash. The air was suddenly filled with AC/DC.

"Seriously "Jailbreak". Really?"

He smiled and I couldn't help but laugh. For the first time since walking through those doors this morning, I felt free. I rolled the window down a couple of inches. The air smelled good. Different. Yeah, I know that's bullshit, but it did.

A few hours later, as we approached Portland, the scenery became familiar as we drove past malls and massive apartment complexes. I spotted the two-story Honda candy store where Jake and I used to hang out and drool until some bored salesman ran us off. On the upper deck, the sun glinted from the chrome on motorcycles and ATVs.

I still felt like a kid looking through a window at something I'd never be able to buy, while Jake could probably walk in and that same salesman would be standing at his shoulder with a latte in one hand and a contract in the other.

Jake reached over and turned up the radio. It

was impossible to talk over the music, which was great until Jake turned left instead of right off Arthur. I had a room in a house over on Halpern a social services agency arranged. "Hey, you're going the wrong way," I shouted over the music. Jake just shrugged and gave me a sort of crooked smile. Or I think he did. It was hard to catch his expression given the thick beard he was sporting.

We pulled into a residential neighborhood and then pulled into the left-side driveway of a duplex. It was a squat tan stucco building with the usual copycat symmetry of most duplexes. There were identical white doors and big picture windows, also trimmed in white. At either end were open carports. The one on the right was empty, and the one on the left held a car under a gray cloth cover.

Jake shut off the car and the sudden silence was jarring.

"What's this?" I asked though I had my suspicions.

"Your new place."

"Jake, you can't—"

"What, pay back my debts?" Jake asked, turning

to look at me with a don't-fuck-with-me expression I couldn't miss, even with the beard. For the first time since he picked me up, I saw the old Jake, the guy I'd grown up with. An abandoned kid who'd turned his hurt into anger and his unmet needs into addiction.

"You paid back any debt years ago," I told him and meant it. "Don't think I didn't appreciate you putting money on my books every month."

"Man can't live on jail food alone."

"True. Ramen and hot sauce are where most of it went, oh, and toothpaste that didn't taste like ass."

"Nice visual. You want to see your place."

"I have a choice?"

Jake didn't say anything, so I gave up—maybe too easily—and opened the car door.

Once inside the apartment, I just sort of stood there with my mouth open. The space had been remodeled and modernized so that the kitchen, dining, and living areas flowed into each other. Open concept they call it. Yes, there was lots of time to watch home improvement shows in jail. The walls were white, and everything else was shades of gray. The kitchen cabinets were light gray to match the concrete countertop of the dining bar. The bar's legs were dark gray, like the row of drop lights, and they, and the row of four brushed-nickel stools tucked under the dining bar, gave the place a slightly industrial feel.

I turned to take in the living room. A gray L-shaped couch faced a dark, slate-tiled fireplace and above it, a huge flat-screen TV. Beyond it, against the far wall, four tall windows with dark gray trim framed a trio of white-barked aspens in the backyard.

"Cassandra?" I asked, hazarding a guess.

Bobby smiled and nodded, "Cassandra, Heather, a couple of others, and even Little Mikey came by, and put in the lights. Don't worry, it wasn't all just for you. I bought the place as an investment, then realized it was handy. Close to Cassandra's place. The other side is set up as a writing space for me. Tax write-off. I use it a couple of times a week, sometimes more. That's why I'd rather have you in here than rent it to somebody with bad habits."

I laughed. "Yeah, wouldn't want that."

Jake smiled, and then with a visible effort,

walked into the living room and put his hand on a thick, blood-red knitted blanket that was draped over the back of the couch. "Zoey made it for me one Christmas," he said. "I figured you might want it."

I nodded. Jake always said Zoey was trouble, but he also knew what he said wouldn't change how I felt about her and that he knew I'd appreciate having something to remind me of her.

I tried to stifle a yawn but couldn't. Knowing I was getting out, I hadn't slept much the last few nights, and I suddenly realized that despite the nap in the car I was bone tired. Jake noticed the way he noticed everything. Probably what's made him a good writer.

"Hey, you take it easy today," he said. There's food in the fridge, Cassandra again, coffee thingy with pods. Instructions are in a drawer. Now, a couple more things I need to show you, and then I'll get out of your way."

He walked into the kitchen and pulled open a drawer, reached in then turned and placed a set of keys on the bar. "House and car," he said, and I saw keys attached to a keychain with a mini pair of fuzzy pink dice. Then he set another keychain down, this one leather with a Yamaha logo. "Keys to the bike," he said.

When I raised my eyebrows at him, he said, "Follow me. I'll show you," and picking up the Yamaha keys he walked across the living room to the left rear corner and a door set there which led to the carport. I followed him out and found, parked in front of the car, and hidden from view when we pulled up, a Yamaha MT-09.

"What's this?" I asked.

"This? This is a motorcycle," he said. "Mo. Tor. Cy. Cle. You remember them, right? I know it's been a while."

"Oh, I remember them," I said. Jake's sarcasm had the wanted effect. I was just annoyed enough to stay quiet. One of two responses to being mad at him that I'd developed over the years.

I stepped up to the bike and without really meaning to, found the palm of my hand on the tank, maybe sort of stroking it like a cat. I made myself stop. Then I noticed the color. "Hey, it's painted to match your car. This is a special bike."

"Well, yeah it is. I keep it here so when I'm here working, I can ride and clear out the cobwebs. Very effective against writer's block, but sadly Cassandra doesn't like me riding a bike and doesn't let me off the leash to ride much anymore."

"Did you guys finally move in together or get engaged or something?"

"Nah." He didn't elaborate, just reached up and tugged at the squared-up Viking beard. I noticed new ink on the back of his hand. The pile of shit and flies he'd put there as a teenager, in an early, and horrifically failed, effort at tattooing had been artfully covered by a compass rose, the kind you find on old maps. It was a vast improvement and I told him so.

"Well, it kind of fits, right? I always was trying to figure out the right direction for me to go."

"But you did," I said, thinking of his success as a writer.

"I guess," he said, but there was doubt in his voice. Then he laughed and said, of course he had, but I'd caught his tone and wondered about it. Well, whatever was bugging him, maybe I could help him figure it out. I owed him, and that was before all this.

"So, are you ready for the big reveal?" he asked.

"What?"

"You want to see the project car I bought you?"

"You bought me a fucking car. Dude, this is too much. Seriously. I'll find a job and get out as soon as—"

"Ah, shut the hell up."

He whipped back the cover and I shut the hell up.

"Hello," I said.

She was up on jacks, no tires, no wheels, just metal, lots, and lots of metal. "I slid my hand along the fender. Seemed I couldn't keep my hands to myself today. "It's not. it can't be Momma Curtis' car." I asked.

"Oh, why can't it?"

The jet-black paint was faded and scratched but the pinstripe was there. That pinstripe was custom. I remembered when Momma Curtis had it applied to her cherry 1966 Dodge Coronet 500. She called the car Princess, joking a coronet was a tiara and that's what a princess wore. She liked to pretend she was unaware of what the sight of that car did to us. The kids from the foster home across the street. But she knew. Oh, she knew. How many times did she *let* me wash that car?

"She die?" I asked, a wave of sadness already hovering.

"Oh, hell no. She just wanted to move to Florida and get out of the rain. Her sister, you remember Lenore, she retired and moved out there first. Probably did it knowing it was the only way to get Momma out of Oregon."

A flash memory of Letitia, Momma's daughter, lit up my brain. Caramel skin, Long agile fingers. The first girl I ever kissed, right there in Momma's backyard. That was maybe one of the bravest or stupidest things I ever did. Momma was fiercely protective of her little girl.

Momma Curtis and her sister, Lenore, ran a foster home for elderly people. Our foster parents, Ann, and Travis Sparrow, lived across the cul-de-sac from them. The traffic between the two houses was nonstop. Momma Curtis was always calling to get one of us kids to either help lift someone into bed or wheel someone down the driveway to a waiting transport van. Momma was always carrying casseroles and pies to our place. Eventually, Lenore bought the house next door and set up a second elder care home. After that, it felt like we owned the whole cul-de-sac.

Jake and I had each lived in a handful of homes, and each had been a horror story of one kind or another. Luckily, we both managed, about six months apart, to end up at the Sparrows. I was fourteen and Jake was thirteen. He was bigger. I was meaner. We got into a fistfight the first week I got there, and I beat him up. Bloodied his nose anyway. After things calmed down, and the blood was washed away, we were ordered to sit out back at the picnic table until dinner.

Most guys would have been mad about getting punched in the nose, but Jake told me he thought I was cool. That I fought like a whirling dervish. That's when we designed my first and only tattoo, a Tasmanian Devil.

We forgot we were supposed to stay put. Ann found us in our shared room, hunched over paper and a comic book, the fight long forgotten. She sighed and left us to it. Ann was cool that way. Travis was more uptight, but they were a good mix for most of us kids. Anyway, they gave half a shit, which is half a shit more than most of the people we'd dealt with in the system.

Despite the bright sun, I felt another yawn coming on. It was a jaw-cracker. "Sorry."

"No need," said Jake. "You hang here and get some rest. I'll call you later."

As we went back inside, I started to tell him I didn't have a phone, but he interrupted and said, "Cass bought you a phone, one of those pay-as-you-go things. It's in the same drawer. I think you have to do something to activate it, but you know her, she would have left instructions."

"Good. I'm supposed to call my PO, let her know where I'm living." I yawned again.

"I'm going already. Don't forget to turn on that phone. We have some things to talk about."

I didn't know what things he meant, and I felt completely talked out. However, as soon as he left the place got weirdly quiet and I kind of wished he'd hung out to talk some more. All that gray, no doubt on trend, reminded me of the concrete cell I'd spent the last year in.

There was a coffee table, a massive wooden thing with steel wheels. More of Cassandra's idea of what a guy like me would want in furniture. It did look sturdy enough to hold an engine block. There was a universal remote sitting on it and I grabbed it and turned on the television.

The five o'clock news was playing. I'd just catch a minute. I sat down. The blanket Zoey knit was right there. I dragged it down. It was soft and made a great pillow. It felt good to stretch out a minute. I closed my eyes.

CHAPTER TWO

I woke up because the sun had shifted and was shining on my face. I sat up slowly, then stretched. My body was a little stiff but otherwise, I felt good. I looked into the kitchen and the microwave told me I'd slept around two hours. It was a little after seven. The TV was droning on, but I didn't really hear it. Getting up, I went in search of a bathroom.

The bathroom held a tub with a shower head as big as a hubcap. There were two sinks in the long counter and between them a basket of toiletries. Probably Cassandra again. I'd have to figure out a way to pay her back. Invite her and Jake over for dinner maybe. I could cook a mean lemon chicken.

After I washed my hands, I opened one of two doors I hadn't tried yet. It revealed a stacked washer and dryer, an unexpected bonus. The second door opened onto a narrow bedroom. At the far end was a double bed flanked by small tables that each held a reading lamp. The curtains were dark gray and the bedspread a simple gray and white stripe. Along the wall to my left were built-in drawers and a row of sliding barnyard doors.

I slid one aside to find a mechanical room with a water tank and furnace. The other three doors concealed a long narrow clothes closet. It wasn't empty. On wooden hangers were new jeans, three gray t-shirts, and several button-down shirts in several shades of blue, one light yellow, one tan. There was an envelope safety-pinned to one of the pairs of jeans. Inside was a note.

Hi Bobby! Hope these fit. Socks and underwear in the dresser. Shoes you can't buy for someone so here's a preloaded credit card. Can't wait to see you.
Love, Heather

She'd drawn a heart underneath or maybe some lips. The ink had smeared, and it was hard to tell

Heather was one of the foster sisters who passed through the Sparrow's house. I think she was there for almost a full year. She told us her previous foster home had been great, but her foster mom got cancer and died. Heather had been older than us by several years but didn't act it. She was always silly and sweet to everyone. They said she was developmentally delayed. I think that's the politically correct way to say it.

She'd been deprived of oxygen in the womb, something about the cord being wrapped around her neck. Her parents hadn't wanted a "dumb" child so had put her into the system. They never knew what they missed.

Heather was a little slow with schoolwork. Math was her nemesis, but she had an eye for quality and design. She fought her way through school and ended up a buyer for a big-name store. Then, after she thought she knew enough, she opened a boutique in Portland. She slept on an REI cot in the backroom, took sponge baths in the sink, and ate only microwavable meals for two years. Then, Coquelicot took off. I'd heard the first thing she did was hire an accountant. No more math.

I was still not sure how to handle all the generosity but knowing Heather I was grateful she'd stuck with the basics.

I heard a knock at the front door and spun around. Who knew I was here? Had to be Jake. Funny how being in a strange place can make you jumpy.

As I was passing through the living room, I saw the picture. It hung in the corner beside the picture window. Someone had cropped an old photograph into a tall rectangle, blown it way up, and had it framed. The central subject of the shot was me, at about sixteen. I had a soccer ball in my hands and was smiling right into the camera. My light brown hair was dark with sweat, and there were grass stains on my knees.

Behind my left shoulder, closer to the house, Jake and one of the temporaries—what we called kids who weren't around for long—were playing some version of touch football. Behind my right shoulder, on the back patio at the picnic table, were Zoey, Letitia, and a girl whose name I couldn't remember. Letitia and the girl were looking at a book open on the table in front of them. Zoey was staring at me with those eyes.

I'd have to check it out later. I resisted the urge to peek through the window and opened the door. Of course, it was Jake.

"Did you try to call?" I asked. "Just got up. Haven't turned on the phone yet."

"I figured as much. Hungry?" he asked and looked down at the pizza box he was holding.

"Hell yeah. Get in here."

We pulled out stools, ate pizza, and drank the beer some kind soul had put in the fridge.

I told Jake I saw the photo.

"Heather did that," he told me. "When we started working on the place, she and Cass put their heads together trying to figure out what kind of art you'd like."

"This was some production."

Jake didn't disagree. We took our beers and wandered over to look at the photograph.

"Where is she?" I asked again, in a casual way that didn't even fool me.

Jake shrugged. "I honestly don't know. Like I said, I think maybe Mexico. When she called, I could hear people in the background. Sounded like Spanish. Hell, could be she's in Spain."

"You always keep in touch with everyone . . ." I said, and left it there, not wanting to come out and accuse him of lying to me.

"When they want to stay in touch. Zoey isn't ready. She'll call when she is."

"No big deal," I said. "Just a habit I guess, worrying about her. Let's get back to my welcome home. What the hell, Jake? I mean, I appreciate it, I really do, but an apartment? A car? A bike? It's too much. And speaking of bikes. Any idea what happened to mine?"

'The one you left at Zoey's?"

"Uh, yeah. The only one."

"Zoey's husband wasn't in the hospital forever. My guess is he took a sledge to it. The pictures I saw made it seem likely that was the weapon of choice."

"Ah, there were pictures?"

"Zoey sent them. She felt bad. Wanted to know if we could put Humpty Dumpty together again."

"That would be a no?"

"That would be a no." Jake agreed.

"I put some miles on that bike," I said.

We went silent for a moment, and I realized Jake understood how I regretted that my actions led to the death of a good bike. A reliable friend, or anyway, a good companion. For a moment I thought about the summer road trip I'd taken when I got out of the service.

Funny how that summer getaway turned into three years. I'd ridden a lot of miles and seen a lot of places as I drove without clear direction across the United States and into Canada. I'd made some friends, human ones, met some women, and gained some good memories. Not really the time to think about it though.

"Look, Jake, I appreciate all this. Seriously, I do, but it's too much. I already have a place to stay, and I'll find work. Mechanics are always in demand. It's great,

The bike, the car. But it's not necessary. I don't even have the money to buy the tools to work on the car."

"Oh, don't worry about that," he said. "The trunk's full of tools. Mikey picked them out. Damn, you don't look so good."

It was true. Suddenly, I felt like I was on overload. Like the edges were too sharp and the room was swaying. I couldn't catch my breath.

"Sit your ass down," Jake said and took the beer out of my hand. I walked over to the couch and did as he said, then leaning forward, my forearms resting on my knees, I waited for the world to return to normal. Deep breaths. Slow. Easy.

"Drink."

I sat up and Jake handed me a glass of something. The smell of good bourbon cut the fog. I took a sip. It burned a little, but I didn't let that slow me down. I tossed the drink back and coughed. It had been a while. The sharp taste turned into instant warmth in my stomach.

Jake was holding the bottle. He poured me another double and then put the bottle back in the kitchen. I was impressed. Not too many years before he'd have joined me. A beer wouldn't have done it. Of course, alcohol had never been his first drug of choice.

"Look, I want you to stay here and work on the car," he said. "The car is yours, a present. The bike you can give back once the car is running. The apartment you can start paying rent on once you get a job. If you want to pay the others back, you have to deal with them. If you want to pay me back you can, with money, or by doing me a favor. "

Sipping the bourbon, panic attack gone but not forgotten, I asked, "What favor?"

"Well, it's for Letitia and Tilly, actually."

"Anything for Letitia, but who's Tilly? I don't think I know her."

"Sure you do. She's in the photograph, sitting with Zoey and Letitia. Matilda Barker."

"Oh yeah, sure, now I remember. The quiet girl. She stayed with us for like, what, three or four months?"

"Yeah, it wasn't long. But she and Letitia got close, like real close."

"Close?" I asked, homing in with my super sleuth skills on what Jake was so subtly trying to convey.

"You knew Letitia is bi, right?"

"I did not. I thought, for a while there, she was all about me." I admitted. "Oh, my fragile male ego."

"Is in no danger," Jake assured me. "Anyway, she and Tilly are a couple now and they need help. I think you might be the person who could help them."

"Moi?" Then, more seriously, "What kind of trouble?"

"They had a business deal with some guy. He broke the deal and took their stuff. They want it back."

"Why don't they go to the cops," I asked, though I thought I already knew the answer. If they hadn't gone to the cops, whatever they were involved in had to be shady.

"Because their stuff is a shit load of weed," said Jake, confirming my guess.

"Weed," I laughed. "Well, that's some low-level shit. Isn't it legal now?"

"Not in the quantity they were moving. That guy took them for a bundle."

"How much are we talking?"

"Not a truckload, but a respectable amount. Letitia says it was packaged to go to a distributor in quarter pound bags, one hundred of them."

I found myself whistling between my teeth. "A QP is what, like nine hundred, maybe a thousand dollars. That's up around a hundred thousand. Are they threatening them?" I asked.

"Threatening them. Who?" Jake asked.

"Their supplier. You know, whoever owns the weed."

Jake laughed. "Do you not remember Letitia or Momma Curtis at all? Momma Curtis didn't raise no fool. Letitia *is* the supplier. She owns the grow, and the guys who work there, work for her. Hell, I think Tilly started out working for her. So, no, it's nothing like that.

"Letitia said she first got into growing marijuana to help a girlfriend with cancer. A medical thing. Then she realized her business degree was more useful, and the business more lucrative, than the entry-level job she had. When weed got legal she did some under-the-table supplying to the legit stores at first, until the monitoring got too good. Now she supplies high-end product to people too rich and impatient—or too anonymous—to walk into a store with a big freaking marijuana leaf on the door."

"Good for her," I told him. "We always knew she'd make it. That's no surprise. What I am surprised by is you needing my help finding this person. I mean. I've been away a long time and you've been here. You must know a ton of people."

Jake shook his head. "Not really. Not anymore. Since I got discovered," He said it like the word tasted bad. "I've been running from one talk show to podcast, to book signing. Seriously, the only thing I don't do is write. Doesn't matter. I promised a long time ago to keep an eye on the family and I will, no matter how busy I am, or where I am. That's why I'm hoping you can help me with this."

I nodded as if I understood. But I didn't really. I'd never completely understood Jake's hero complex. Maybe it was all those comics we read as kids—and still read. For whatever reason, to Jake, the kids who lived with us at the Sparrow's, no matter how long they stayed, no matter what shits they were, were family.

Even though our backgrounds were different, the reasons we got dumped into foster care were different, we both knew family was important. It was just that we didn't agree on what an obligation to family meant. For Jake, if someone was family, they fell under the umbrella of his protection. He'd do anything for them. Need a ride? Call Jake. Need help moving? Call Jake. Need bail? Jake.

This fierce loyalty to family, for some reason, didn't seem to extend to his girlfriend, Cassandra. At least not to that same level of commitment. It was strange. I knew he was crazy about her, and she was good for him. All I could think of was that she'd had a traditional childhood. A loving family. A normal progression of school, college, job, and upward mobility. She didn't share his darkness, so maybe she didn't work so well as his muse.

Until Cassandra, each of Jake's girlfriends had been what I'd call a hot mess, and that's being nice. He was big into rescuing women who didn't want to be rescued. Jake was famous for his novels. Dark thrillers about broken people. People who managed to make it chapter by chapter all the way to the end, but the journey was on their knees over broken glass.

Cassandra seemed happy. I thought a happy woman, that kind of light, could burn away the darkness he carried. Maybe it could also burn away what made his writing special. That's the kind of thing I did with the free hours in my cell, analyzed my friends like bugs under a magnifying glass.

I raked my fingers through my hair and said, "What you're saying, to be clear, is all I have to do is find some guy who ripped Letitia and Matilda off for a hundred thousand in weed, return it to her, and you and I are square?"

"No. We're square anyway. What I'm saying is the girls need help and also, there's a fifty percent finder's fee on the deal."

"Fifty percent? Fifty percent of . . . ?"

"Here, let me do the math for you. Fifty percent of one hundred thousand is fifty thousand dollars. Are you interested now?"

"Well, I don't know Jake," I said, shaking my head soberly. That kind of money? I wouldn't know what to do with it. As you know, I'm just a Poe boy from a Poe family."

Jake shook his head. "Ah fuck, I wondered when you'd get around to that. I'm glad you're back, you asshole."

"Me too," I said, and I meant it.

CHAPTER THREE

The favor Jake wanted me to do for him felt like the kind of thing you'd hire a detective for. So, what would a detective do I wondered? Maybe, talk to people, ask questions? I found the phone Cassandra bought me, used a steak knife to saw it free of the plastic package, and then plugged it in to charge. While it was charging, I decided to take a shower and see if the clothes Heather had bought for me fit.

The soap and shampoo her or Cassandra selected were a hell of a lot better than I was used to. There were suds. I toweled off with one of the thick towels and stalked naked into the bedroom in search of underwear. As promised, I found two neatly folded piles of both boxers and briefs. Nice to give me choices.

I selected navy blue briefs then found the sock drawer and again went with dark blue.

The jeans were a little stiff. A few washings would take care of that. Being a rebel, I skipped the row of blue shirts and took the lone yellow one. I would have to check out my storage locker soon. I'd left a duffle bag of clothes there before heading out on my trip. There was also a flat-screen television, parts and tires for my old bike, a file box of important papers like my birth certificate, past taxes, and other proof of adultness. More importantly, I'd also left my rifle, two handguns, ammo, and a collection of knives locked inside a footlocker. Given the kind of person I suspected I'd be looking for, I might just need them. Maybe Jake or Heather would run me out there so I could get my stuff moved. Might as well save money on storage. If this fifty percent recovery fee didn't pan out, I'd be in trouble. I was short on savings, and I was not going to take another penny from Jake.

The phone was charged and as soon as I turned it on it started vibrating. There was a ten-minute-old text from Jake telling me Letitia and Tilly wanted to meet with me. Could I come over? I texted back that of course I could.

I shoved my feet in my boots and laced up, then grabbed my jacket, old and as soft as I wished the jeans were. Last, I went into the kitchen and found the Yamaha key ring.

The bike was different. It took a minute, but by the time I left Beaverton and crossed into Portland, we were friends.

Jake's place was off Skyline Boulevard on a single lane with maybe four houses along it. Each was set back from the road, so it was hard to see them. Mailboxes at the end of each driveway marked the addresses or I might have missed it. It had been some time since I'd been there.

I pulled up to the house, which was an older Craftsman, all rock and cedar with a porch both deep and wide and noticed the new garage. It was bigger than the house and though younger, you couldn't tell because it had been sided to match. It stood to the left of the house and farther back on the lot. In front of its two roll-up doors was a powder blue Fiat, Cassandra's or Letitia's was my guess.

Letitia basically jumped me at the door, exclaiming about how great I looked and dragging me into the house. "Ooh don't take the coat off," she said. "I love a man in leathers. Nummy."

We ended up in the living area on one of two leather couches that faced each other in front of a fireplace big enough to roast a steer. As soon as I sat down Letitia bounced down between me and the arm of the couch and Tilly plopped down on my other side. Immediately Letitia swung her legs over mine, putting her bare feet in Tilly's lap.

So much female company. Damn. Letitia was sexy as ever. She always reminded me of a cat. Slender, with a long torso and fluid graceful fingers. Even her toes were long and thin and somehow hot.

Tilly was better looking than I remembered, with red hair and a dancer's body. She wasn't quite as comfortable with me as Letitia was but was trying to play along.

Letitia wriggled her butt against my leg, obviously to tease Tilly. Tilly ignored her, reached for an old-fashioned cigarette roller on the big oak coffee table, and began to roll a joint.

Jake came in with four beers in long-neck bottles and handed one to each of us before settling on the other couch.

"Where's Cassandra?" I asked.

Jake looked at me like I'd lost my mind. "She's a lawyer," he reminded me. "Officer of the court?"

I felt like an ass. Of course, she wouldn't be here to hear us plan something just shy of, okay way shy of, legal. I nodded like a wise old sage and took a good pull of the beer. Not bad. I turned it so I could read the label. Dead Guy Ale, Rogue Brewery. I couldn't help but smile. Perfect choice for a writer of dark thrillers.

Tilly handed me the joint and I took a couple of hits off it before handing it to Letitia. She looked at it in her hand, and sounding like a snooty sommelier said, "A very mellow variety, outdoors, low THC, almost vintage. Perfect for relaxing but staying sharp. You feeling sharp Bobby boy?"

"Never sharper, Let. Never sharper."

"Well, that ain't sayin' much but I don't got much choice."

It always amused me when Letitia spoke as if the rules of grammar had suddenly fallen out of her head.

Especially since she was the one that got me through most of my English classes. Or maybe everything was amusing because I wasn't sitting in a cell, or maybe the THC was already tickling through my brain cells. I gave her another of my wise sage looks and said, "Tell me all about this person you'd like me to find for you."

"Right to business, huh? I guess that works for me. I first met this guy through a legit contact. They backed him completely. He was okay. I mean, he wasn't big on sharing. I don't even know his real name. He had me call him Mr. B. I was okay with that because, like I said, he was recommended to me by someone I trusted. On their good word, I sold him a couple of bags the first time, then ten, then twenty a couple of times. Maybe eighty bags total over a year and a half. This time though, he upped it a lot. Said he'd found another buyer."

"And you didn't question that?"

"Why would I? I didn't ask or care who his buyer was. It's not like he was subleasing my apartment or something. Anyway, he showed up for the pickup as usual but this time he had two armed thugs with him.

They locked me and Tilly in a closet, loaded up the product, and took off."

"I broke a nail picking the lock," Tilly said, holding out her hands to show that her purple fingernails had been trimmed short.

"You poor thing," I said in what I hoped was a supportive tone.

"Don't encourage her," Letitia said. "What are you going to do?"

I shrugged. "Ask you some more questions. Then go find someone else to ask more questions. Don't know any other way to find stuff out."

The doorbell rang. I looked at Jake, who was getting up. "I ordered Chinese. Should we move this party into the dining room?"

"We should," said Letitia.

"Chinese food makes Letitia horny," Tilly gleefully informed us.

Tilly was not the quiet girl I once knew.

By the time I ate, drank too much, then sobered up enough to drive back to my place it was late. I was tired but couldn't sleep. It was too quiet. Strangely, the silence intensified every small creak and groan of the place. When the furnace kicked in it woke me up from the doze I'd managed. The sound of a car driving by did the same.

Finally, I realized I was missing the noise of the place I'd been living in for the last year. I got up took a pillow with me, turned on the TV, laid on the couch with Zoey's afghan over me, and with the distant hum of voices, slept like a rock.

I woke up with a plan. In my restlessness, I'd done some thinking. I had two avenues. Lying there wide awake I listed them.

First, I should call Howie. He was a friend, a mechanic, who worked for O. H. Rose Limo. The guy who owned the business, Oliver Rose, was a bona fide criminal element. Howie had told me a few things. Nothing specific that I could use if say, I wanted to speak with law enforcement, but enough. Howie was like one degree from Kevin Bacon. If anything criminal was going on in our little corner of the planet, then Oliver Rose would probably know about it. Maybe he'd even heard about something as inconsequential as Letitia getting burned. It was a remote possibility but the best I could come up with. Maybe Howie would have some other ideas to add to mine.

The second thing I'd do is find and talk to Andy Kapland. Andy was a Portland local who, by some strange confluence of circumstances, had also found himself in Crescent City, California a guest of the local jail, at the same time I had.

This commonality of geography gave us things to talk about. We'd discuss our basketball team, the Blazers, the local comedian and celebrity, Fred Armisen, the chance of scoring with a Rose Festival Princess, zero, and other Portland-specific things. If Howie and his connections couldn't help, maybe Andy and his could.

Since I'd lost my phone, I didn't have any numbers, but the limo company was listed. With luck he'd still be working there. Luck was with me. One transfer later I heard a familiar voice.

"It's the shop. What you need?"

"What do you think I need?"

"Bobby. Goddam. Bobby Fucking Poe? You in town?"

"I am. Was hoping to talk to you."

"Sure. You want to hang out, maybe grab some dinner?"

"Sounds good."

"You want me to come get you?"

"No. I have a ride."

"You want to meet at Murphy's, at say 5:30?"

"You bet."

"Bobby Fucking Poe. Damn." Then he hung up.

A better reception than I'd expected. It had been a while since I'd seen Howie or anyone from the old days. Three years on the road had left a gap. I hadn't really expected Howie to still be working for Oliver. Guess not everyone had to keep moving. I looked at the phone. Now for the tricky part. How would I find Andy?

I decided to think about it while taking a trip to my storage shed to pick up a few things.

I dug through most of the boxes I'd left there but all I ended up doing was rearranging the piles. Can't carry much on a bike. All I brought back was two hundred dollars I'd stashed, two of my favorite knives, a Glock 17, and a box of ammo. The gun made me think of a particular memory from when I first started hanging around with Howie.

One afternoon, not long after meeting him, he and I had been working on his car. He had to wait for a part so we couldn't finish. Since he was carless, he asked if I could give him a ride to pick up some weed. I said sure, and we drove to a mobile home park. Though I wanted to stay in the car, Howie insisted I come in and be sociable.

Once inside I met the sellers, an older couple, maybe in their late sixties or early seventies. The wife was sitting in a recliner with a TV table in front of her, painting on a small canvas. I could see she was trying to concentrate but she was too polite to ignore me and asked if I'd like some tea or coffee while I waited. I said no thanks and she asked me to sit down, which I did, sitting on the edge of the couch while Howie and her husband headed down a hallway to the back of the house.

We were sitting there, in this sort of awkward silence when I heard the unmistakable sound of a rifle bolt being pulled back. My stomach filled with ice, and I got to my feet fast. The old lady didn't react to the sound, but she did give me a funny look when I shot up like that. Maybe she was going deaf or something. It didn't matter. All I was thinking about was whether to run for the door or run to the back room to help Howie.

That's when I saw him coming down the hall with the old man right behind him. Both were laughing like nothing had happened, except maybe the telling of a good joke. I swallowed my stomach back into place, or at least that's what it felt like.

"What the fuck was that?" I asked as soon as we got in the car.

"What?"

"The sound of a rifle being cocked. I thought the old man was going to shoot you."

"Oh that," he waved away my concern. "He bought a new deer rifle and was showing it off to me. Did you hear that out in the living room?"

"Yes, I fucking heard that, and you owe me a new pair of underwear."

He laughed but I didn't. I wasn't amused and wasn't even going to pretend to be. To this day I remember the sensation, the fear that swept over me when I heard that sound. I shake it off, as I always do. I've been in worse spots, real trouble, but somehow the oily slide and click of that bolt being drawn still shows up in my nightmares from time to time. Might be why the feeling of that gun tucked into a holster and clipped at the small of my back felt so foolishly reassuring.

By the time I got back to the duplex I still hadn't come up with any brilliant ideas. I parked the bike and went inside. Pulling out the leftover pizza, I set about nuking some lunch. Maybe Jake would have an idea or three for finding Andy. Might as well call and ask. One thing about writers, they know how to find out stuff.

I gave Jake everything I knew about Andy and decided that was the best I could do until after my meeting with Howie.

I finished lunch, tidied up, probably the only good habit I'd picked up from my Army days, grabbed the keys, and headed out to see what presents were waiting in Momma's old car.

The trunk was loaded with stuff, but the crowning glory was a red Snap-On toolbox filled to the brim. Thousands of dollars' worth of tools. Fucking Jake.

Fucking Mikey too. Across the top of the box Mikey had used a stencil to spray paint in big black letters, and not too neatly, Bobby's Toy Box.

I couldn't resist and spent the rest of the afternoon working on Princess. The first order of business was getting a battery hooked up so the radio would work. Can't work without tunes. The second was to come up with a better name.

Around four I shut things down, grabbed a shower, then took off for Murphy's. The bar was in Northeast Portland, not far from the famous Saturday Market. I parked and went in. Howie was already there, a short man I'd heard called the Danny DeVito of pulling wrenches. He was seated at a table in a far corner on the bar side of the place. Good. The smaller table for four, tucked out of the way, was perfect for the questions I had to ask.

"Hey, you made it. Grab a seat," Howie said, Then he signaled to a waitress who hurried over. She got there so fast I figured he was either a good tipper or she knew who he worked for. Either way, I was happy to give my order for Guinness and shepherd's pie. Howie ordered the same.

"They have a single malt here." He brought his fingers together and made a kissing noise. A very Italian gesture from a guy who I knew was born and raised in Seattle, Washington. "Straight from Ireland. We'll have to get a sample after we eat. Now tell me what you've been up to since last time I seen you."

As with everyone else in my life, the last time had been three years ago. A lot had happened in that time, and I didn't know where to start. I was glad when he of started for me.

"I heard from Jake you were in jail for beating some guy into the ground. If it was like that beat down you delivered to that Jason dick, back in the day. I still owe you for that, by the way. Anway, from what I heard, it must have been epic."

I wanted to tell him he didn't owe me anything. It was Howie's stuff that was stolen, but the trunk of the car the kid messed up with a crowbar had been mine. It had been just as much my business as it was his. However, considering I was about to ask for a favor it seemed like a bad idea to say so. Instead, I flipped his question. "What have *you* been doing the last few years? I'm surprised you're still working at Rose's."

"Ten years and then some," he bragged. "Yeah, it's a good job and I'm in no hurry to leave. Got a 401k and an IRA both. Putting a few bucks in every chance I get. One of these days my old body will be too beat up to work and I'll want that island money."

"You still want to retire to Hawaii?"

"Sure, that's the plan."

I had a hard time imagining Howie leaving the life he'd created. For a man just an inch or so over five-foot-tall he commanded a lot of respect around here from the people who shared the semi criminal lifestyle he'd chosen to embrace. Maybe in Hawaii, he'd go totally legit and not need a reputation, but it was unlikely.

Our food and beer came. Howie ordered a refill before even touching his. This was going to take a dent out of my two hundred seventeen and change but it would be worth it. Murphys was famous for their good beer and excellent shepherd's pie.

We caught up between bites. The second round of beer showed up just when it was needed. The place was getting packed, and the dull roar was nice. Then, from the corner of my eye, I caught some motion and looked up. Two overdressed women, one black, one white, wearing short dresses and high heels had strolled in and were walking up to our table. They passed me by and went to stand behind Howie.

The white one bent down and near his ear in a fake whisper said, "This your friend?"

Howie smiled at me and said, "Excuse my bad manners. Girls, this is Bobby Poe. *The* Bobby Poe, and Bobby this is Gracey, he nodded toward the black girl, and Lacey," he said, indicating the white one. "Come on, sit down, girls."

They did. Lacey next to Howie. Gracey next to me. I shot a quizzical eyebrow at Howie.

"The girls work for Rose Limo," he explained.

Based on their clothes and their makeup I'd guessed that. What I was wondering was why they were at our table. I didn't have enough in my pockets for half an hour with either one of them. Howie saw my distressed look and said, "Let's have a drink. Then we're gonna go for a ride."

"Drinks!" The girls enthused. Lacey even clapped her hands.

Howie gestured for the waitress and when she arrived, he ordered two shots of the Irish single malt he'd mentioned, a bottle of white wine, and two champagne flutes. The girl's preferred kind of glassware, he explained. A few minutes in I realized why. Lacey had this way of sliding her long fingers and manicured nails up and down the narrow glass. Gracey liked to slide her tongue along the edge of her glass as she lifted it to drink. Both things had me doing some readjusting in my seat.

When we finished the first bottle of wine, Howie told me dinner was on him and wouldn't even let me tip. I was learning my friends were all generous, almost to a fault. I was starting to understand what the fault part of that expression meant. Howie tossed the cost of dinner, plus a twenty on the table and we got out of there.

An O.H. Rose Company Limo was parked across the street, taking up two spaces. In a cloud of perfume, flanked by the two women, I followed Howie, a willing puppet, across the street and into the back seat.

"Let's go for a ride, shall we folks?"

I nodded and climbed in after Gracey.

The back of the limo had an L-shaped leatherette couch and a full bar. The windows were blacked out and dark as twilight. A row of tiny lights in the ceiling gave an intimate feel to the place. So did Lacey's hand on my thigh.

The window between the back of the limo and the driver was down. Howie looked back and said, "Have fun, kids."

After a moment the window slid up, also darker than the night, and "Love Removal Machine" by The Cult started to play from speakers all around us. First Jake and now this. My friends were all trying to be the DJs of my life.

Gracey reached across to the bar, flipped open a hinged leather-covered lid, and pulled out a chilled bottle of wine like a magician pulling a rabbit out of a hat. "Want some?" she asked. I shook my head no. She poured two drinks, quickly and expertly, this time into tall wine glasses. She ticked one long nail against a rose etched into the glass. "Oh Fuckin' rose," she said

I'd heard O.H. Limo called that before, but never in a tone filled with so much bitterness.

A moment later Gracey was smiling warmly at me, and I wondered if I'd imagined her anger. The limo backed up smoothly, but Gracey spilled a little of the wine. Both women giggled, and she licked it off her wrist. These women liked their wine, and they knew their business. With one hand wrapped around her glass, Lacey was somehow able to use her other to ease my zipper down.

"I don't know about this," I said. "What if Howie gets curious."

They both laughed, and then Gracey showed me a small remote. "We have all the control. He can be as curious as he likes and too bad. Besides, he's not a voyeur. Make you feel better to hold it?" she asked, holding the remote out to me.

"No, I'm good," I told her. "Reassured that whatever was about to happen wasn't going to be part of a peep show was all I needed to hear. Plus, Lacey had managed to get the zipper all the way down and was now working on the button. "Let me get that," I told her. "Wouldn't want you to break a nail."

"Now that is damn thoughtful," said Gracey. She took Lacey's glass and slid both into a holder on the bar. Then, the two women gave me their undivided attention.

CHAPTER FOUR

Eventually, the girls got fresh drinks and lowered the partition so I could tell Howie it was time to head home for the evening. He didn't say much, or rib me, which was a relief. Working for Oliver had probably taught him a lot about discretion.

Once we pulled into the restaurant's parking lot I got out and so did Howie, leaving the girls inside. Howie walked with me toward my bike.

"That was. Well, that was something." I said finally and a little awkwardly.

"Sure," Howie said, with a whatever shrug of his shoulders. "Hey, I figured you been in jail awhile. The girls owe me a favor or five."

"Do they?"

"Sure. I drive two nights a week, and they want to do a little freelance, I look the other way. They have a couple of regulars that don't get on the books."

"Sounds like a good arrangement."

"It is. Not gonna last long though. Both those gals are hardcore alcoholics. They stick with wine when they work, or Oliver would send them up north."

"Seattle?" I guessed.

"Alaska. The cold hell of hookers."

"You sure know a lot of strange things. Look, I have a favor I need to ask you and I know you need to get rolling so I guess I'll come right out with it."

"Sure, what is it?"

"I'm trying to help a friend who got burned on a deal on some weed. The guy took a hundred QP bags which isn't nothing. Someone has to be talking about it. Did you hear anything?"

He paused, as if he was thinking about it then said, "Afraid not. At least, not yet. This recent?"

"Very."

"Oliver might know something."

"You think you could ask him?"

"Sure. No problem. I'll go over to the office and talk to him in the morning."

"You sure it won't cost you, piss him off or anything?"

"To ask a question? Come on. He's not a psycho like his brother. No. If he doesn't want to answer he won't. We have a good relationship. After ten years with him? Come on."

"That's good. I did hear some bad stuff about his brother. Guess that's what made me nervous. So, I heard right, he is a little crazy?"

"A little . . . Look, saying Hugh Rose is a little crazy is like saying Moses Brown is a little tall. Yeah, he's a full on psycho and quirky as shit. Puts on airs. You ever hear Oliver talk? Sounds like he was born here. Hugh always has just a little bit of that British accent, likes to remind you where he comes from. It's funny because they've both been in the US like twenty years, right? You'd expect them to talk the same."

"Maybe Hugh likes British TV?"

Howie laughed. "Sure. As good a reason as any. All I know about their history is they were running women someplace in the UK and got in trouble. When they got to the US, they found out Portland was called the Rose City. They thought, given their last name is Rose, that it was a sign from God or something. So, they started O.H. Rose Limos and maybe they were right because they've done pretty well for themselves."

"I hear they have a lot of side gigs."

"Well, Oliver just runs the women and car parts. You knew that. Hugh, he's into heavier shit, drugs, and loans. Some kind of angel investing stuff I think is money laundering stuff, but I don't understand half of it, and I don't want to. I'm happy with my job. I help Oliver when I can, fix some mileage here or there, take a special client to a meeting, and keep my mouth shut. Same things I've always done. Oliver's good people. He treats everyone fair. He knows I deal a little Oxy on the side sometimes, mostly to busted up construction workers, and he's never checked me on it. He knows people have to work, gotta eat."

"I'm glad to hear it. You call or text me if you find out he knows something, okay?" I'd given him my number earlier, while we were having dinner.

"I will. Probably have something for you tomorrow but I'll let you know either way."

"Thanks, Howie, and thanks." I raised my chin to point toward the limo.

"Oh damn," he said, jumping visibly. "I better get those girls to work. I like them. They're smart and they got a good thing going. The whole black girl, white girl thing, they came up with that themselves. Pretty popular and safer working as a team. Can't leave them alone though. The bar's probably drunk dry by now. Shit. I'll talk to you soon."

Then he was off, striding across the lot with purpose and a certain swagger.

On the way home I decided to exit onto the highway and open the bike up a little. I could feel every bump of the asphalt surface, rushing by five inches below my boots. The wind battered my chest, my arms felt heavy and my hands cold. Everything was so immediate. I blew by big rigs, slapped by their slipstream, and lit up by their headlights. I moved carefully between cars, steel cages, with drivers oblivious to the nearness of death and the fact of their mortality.

I had to concentrate on every movement, every nuance of the road, and the traffic. I had to be in the moment. No time to think. Just move. Lean. Pass the moron on his phone weaving across the center line. Watch the Dodge Charger with the temporary registration whose driver is playing leapfrog, trying to see what his new ride can really do. Look at the gauges and realize you're doing ninety-eight in a fifty-five. Bring it down slowly. No cops. Breathe. Find the exit and start moving over. Try to stop smiling because you look like an idiot.

I couldn't help myself. It had been a good day.

In the morning the phone chirped. A text from Jake.

Brunch here? Me and Cassandra? 11:00.

Sounds good. I texted back. I had nothing to report but I suspected the brunch wasn't about that. It was probably more about getting to know Cassandra, whom I'd only met a couple of times. About all I knew was that Jake had met her when she'd been working on some copyright problem for one of the authors at his publishers. I didn't know much about how it worked but I gathered publishing houses picked certain books or authors and helped promote and protect them. Apparently, that included hiring lawyers. Cassandra was that kind of lawyer. It sounded like the most boring work in the world but then what job wasn't?

Today I chose one of the blue button-down shirts. For the first time, I noticed my boots were getting a little rough. Maybe I should use the credit card Heather left for me. Maybe forget the boots. Some Nikes or Adidas would be a nice change. Jake had always been a Converse guy, black or red. As kids, we'd had long debates about these all-important choices.

When I pulled up Jake's driveway and parked in front of his garage there was a kind of uncomfortable vibe that pulsed through me. A sense of the serf visiting his lord kind of thing. It was stupid and I knew it. Jake would be pissed if I told him how I felt right then but how could it be any different? The balance between us was way off. I had to get this favor done, pay him back, and swing the balance back the other way a little.

As I got off the bike, took off my helmet and hung it up I tried to remember Cassandra. As I recalled she seemed pretty buttoned up and very serious. Jake had said she was a lawyer and she had looked just like my idea of what a lawyer would look like. At least she sure dressed like one. Nice matching outfit, sensible heels. A brunette with shoulder-length hair pushed behind her ears, and dark-rimmed glasses. Not bad looking but not special either. Jake saw something in her though. Maybe it was that she had all her teeth, or that she had read more than one book. Hard to know what the attraction was, and not my business anyway.

I left the past and came back to the now. The sun was climbing, and already putting out that mid-summer heat. It felt good. I rolled my shoulders and then walked toward the house.

I knocked and Jake yelled, "Come in," so I did. Then, taking a not-too-hard guess at where he was, I walked through the living room, down a short hallway, and into the kitchen at the back of the house, drawn, unerringly, toward the scent of bacon.

Cassandra was sitting on a ladderback chair pulled up to an enormous old farm table in the center of the room. She had on jean shorts and a white tank with spaghetti straps, one of which had slipped off her lightly freckled shoulder. She was holding a wine glass full of something that looked like orange juice, but from the flush on her cheeks, and the champagne bottle on the table was probably a mimosa.

Jake had his back to me, busy at the stove. He turned his head and said, "Hey. Glad you made it. Food's almost ready." Then he turned back to what he'd been doing.

"Hi, Bobby," Cassandra said. "I just made a pitcher. You want one?"

"Sure," I said and watched her pour. This was not the woman I remembered meeting three years ago. This one seemed the opposite of buttoned-up. She was barefoot and bare-legged, and those legs were long, tanned, and toned. She handed me the drink and I noticed her big brown eyes, the cleft in her chin, and the wide smile. Her hair was tousled like she'd rolled out of bed and run her fingers through it. It was dark brown and silky. Maybe Jake wasn't wrong about the whole librarian lawyer thing.

"You look like you just saw a goat in a grocery store," Cassandra said, as blunt as a hammer.

"Sorry. It's just the last time I saw you, you were wearing a suit," I explained.

"Probably a court day. The uniform of the job. Was I super grim and wearing glasses?"

"I-I think so," I stammered, beginning to feel embarrassed by my initial quick assessment. I was also a little annoyed at myself for the moment of attraction I'd felt, was feeling. A bare shoulder is nice, but not when it belongs to your best friend's girl.

"They make me look smarter," she explained. Then, she gave me this intense look and I could see she was working herself up to something. She picked up her drink, stared into it momentarily, and then back at me. "Look Bobby Poe," she said, "my Jake loves you, so I'm prepared to love you, but we have to set some rules." She took a sip of the mimosa.

"Okay," I said. Wondering where this was going.

"First, it's Cassandra or Cass, never, ever Cassie. Got it?"

"Yes ma'am," I said, warming to the game.

"I can flirt with you, in front of Jake of course, but you do not get to hit on me. Got it?"

"Got it."

"You must promise to always protect Jake. Keep him from doing stupid things and this is important. If you see him hitting on some woman you are to report it to me immediately. This is the basis for our friendship. You are my eyes. You get that?"

"I do."

"Good. I think we're going to be friends. Also, remember this, I may only be a copyright lawyer, but I have lots of friends who are criminal defense attorneys, really good ones."

"I don't think I'll ever need…"

"Just a precaution," she said. "You never know what you need until you need it." She smiled at me again and my impression, that she'd hit the mimosas early and often blew right out of my head. Cassandra was stone-cold sober and serious as a heart attack. She meant exactly what she said. She wanted me to take care of Jake, keep him safe, keep him loyal and she'd pay me back with whatever resources she had. I thought, damn. I had better stay on her good side. She'd be a better friend than an enemy.

"Now, I've gotta pee. Don't eat all the bacon before I get back." She set the nearly full glass on the table and strode away, all long legs and self-assurance.

"Jesus," I said. Not meaning to speak out loud.

"She has that effect. Scary, ain't she?" asked Jake.

"She really is," I replied, unsure if I thought that was good or bad.

While Cassandra was gone, I told Jake about my meeting with Howie, leaving out the trip in the limo with the girls. I mean he was practically married, and it seemed a little cruel to brag.

"While I'm waiting for Howie to get back to me, I figured I might as well try to find Andy. He seemed well-connected and might have heard something. I should have learned more about him when we were in jail. If I had a general idea of where he lived, I could probably find him pretty easily. He wasn't the most low-key guy. Any idea how to find his address?"

"Have you tried using the California Inmates Records search?" Cassandra asked, reentering the room. If your friend was in a California jail or prison, he's probably still in it. It takes a while before they clear the records. The database usually lists names and addresses and all sorts of things you probably don't care about."

Jake and I exchanged concerned looks.

"Oh please, I appreciate how Jake tries to protect me from some of his—activities—but I doubt he'd ever be involved in anything that's not for the good of someone. "Would you, babe?"

"Never."

"Didn't think so. I've got an account. Want me to help?"

I did.

It took Cassandra about four minutes to log in, enter the name, and get a result. Andy's address was in the Powellhurst-Gilbert area of Portland. One of the more interesting or less safe neighborhoods, depending on your perspective. It figured.

"I'm going to head over there," I told them.

"Without eating?" Cassandra asked.

"Of course not," I said. I drank a glass of orange juice, wrapped four slices of bacon in a piece of toast, and made my exit. Cassandra's talk had changed the vibe. The lord and serf bullshit that had been playing in my brain was gone. I was back to just being thankful I had Jake as a bother, and now hopeful that Cassandra would become a friend. Of course, it sounded like she already had plenty of friends, some of them defense attorneys. Interesting.

CHAPTER FIVE

Andy was living in an Oxford house, an addiction recovery home. They were all different and all the same. Meant to house six to ten people, men or women, never a mix of the two. No thirteenth stepping. The thirteenth step is an unofficial rule of AA and NA that suggests that someone less than a year in recovery shouldn't be dating or having sex with anyone, especially someone else in recovery. It put both at risk and you had to be focused on working your program, not on a new relationship.

The Oxford houses were always kept up, yards mowed, and paint freshened up. Most people who got to stay in one were happy to be there and eager for something to do, even house or yard work. For a rare time, they had structure and felt at least a little secure.

Of course, there were always those who were not so happy, usually because they'd been court-ordered to be there. The mix of people could be a positive thing or a negative one and could change from month to month.

This one was two stories, gray, and completely unremarkable. I parked the bike in the otherwise empty driveway. Not too many of the residents could afford cars and if they could they probably weren't allowed to drive anyway. Most people don't know the DMV can take your license for a lot of things, not just driving under the influence. For instance, not paying taxes or court fines or child support. It never made a lot of sense to me to take away someone's way to get to work if they couldn't afford to pay their fines, but hey, I'm not the one who voted for that.

I knocked and a blond guy with a bullet head and a bad attitude let me in. Andy was out back, he said. He hadn't been friendly but at least he hadn't lied. I found Andy sitting in one of six green plastic chairs, arranged around a circle of bricks that made a fire pit. It didn't look like anyone burned much in it except cigarette butts. The thing was basically a giant ashtray. Andy was out there smoking, and I realized there was probably a no-smoking-in-the-house policy.

When Andy heard the door he looked up. Same long face and narrow nose, blue eyes a little close together, straight hair cut short revealing big ears, a small cross worn in each of them. He also had a thin beard and a thinner mustache. A huge, gap-toothed smile lit up his face.

"Dude. Is that Bobby Fucking Poe?"

I was starting to think I had a new middle name.

"How you doing?" I asked him.

He sort of got halfway up to give me a quick fist bump then sank back down. "I'm good. What the heck brings you out here?" he asked. "You moving in?"

"No. Got my own place."

"Good. I mean, I wouldn't be here if I didn't have to be. And shit, sit down."

I took a seat on the edge of one of the plastic chairs. They were big Adirondack things that wanted you to sit deep and lean back and never get up again. "How are you doing?" I asked again.

"Oh, pretty good, I guess. It's been eight weeks. Been hitting meetings. Was trying to do one a day but now I'm maybe three times a week."

"That's not good. You strong enough for that?"

He looked away, then spit into the fire pit. "Shit no, dude. Not strong enough for nothing. You know that."

Andy and I had attended the jail's recovery program, going to meetings, talking the talk, drinking the coffee, and eating the cookies. NA or AA, inside or out, was pretty much the same thing. AIAO we used to call it. Andy made up the acronym. It stood for assholes in, assholes out. For me, being in the program was a way to kill time. Andy was an addict who wanted to get clean, plus he liked being in the treatment dorm because he got to take smoke breaks and hang out with girls. It was coed. Plus, by completing the program there was a good chance he'd get a lot of his time cut.

Without the group, he'd probably have been drinking pruno, jailhouse hooch. It was made from sugar, bread, and water with sometimes some fruit for flavor, all of it left in a warm place while the yeast in the bread combined with the sugars and became alcohol. A ceiling panel above the showers had been the favored place in the facility. If he hadn't been drinking he'd probably have been buying pills. A lot of the guys were good at cheeking their meds, like Vicodin, and selling them.

In the recovery program, I couldn't be his sponsor because I'd never been where he was, but I could be his friend. He told me it helped and that made me feel like I was doing something other than sitting on my hands for twelve months.

He seemed shaky. It wasn't just what he was saying, but the way he couldn't sit still. I recognized that restlessness. I'd seen it in Jake often enough. Next thing Jake would decide he needed something just to calm down. Nothing major, just a little something to take the edge off. A few days later the cops would be picking him up out of an empty lot or an alley behind a bar.

"You know dude, you were always good to me. Remember when you asked me to play handball with you? Nobody ever asked me to do stuff. We kicked ass too."

"Yeah, we did."

"You always treated me like a person."

"You are a person, Andy. What is going on? What's the problem?"

"It's this place," he said, shooting a fearful glance toward the back door. The door was closed but he still leaned close and lowered his voice. "They use. Even—." He looked around again. "Even the president. I think the whole house is gonna fall. It's half there, maybe more than halfway already."

"Shit."

"I know. I can't stay here man. I can't."

"I hear you but, I mean, can't you let them fall alone?"

"You know. Well, maybe you don't. Anyway, it don't work that way. A house falls, it usually falls all the way."

I nodded. I'd heard of it before. One member of an Oxford house starts using, and pretty soon someone else joins in and then it's girlfriends coming over, smoking, drinking. A house fell member by member, like dominoes.

"Maybe if you hit more meetings."

"How? The fucking bus? That's a huge hassle. By the time I walk to the bus stop, I'm sweating, and I stink. Who wants to sit in a meeting like that? Besides, it's not like there's anything I can learn I don't already know. Hell, I can recite the book front to back and back to front. I could teach the fucking thing."

"That's not the point, and you know it. Look, Andy, you told me you used to be the best at what you did. You said until you started using there was no house you couldn't break into. Then you got all messed up and you got caught."

"No dude, that's not what happened. You forgot what I told you. I wasn't messed up. I wanted to *be* messed up, but I didn't have any money. I'd seen this place and I knew they had all kinds of goodies. I rushed it. I needed a fix too bad. Usually, I'd keep an eye on a house like that for a few days. Figure out who came and went and when. Only I broke my pattern and took a chance. Getting in was no problem. I just didn't know the owner's ex-cop brother was staying. He woke up, pulled a gun, and held me for the police. It was shit luck.

"Yeah, I remember now. That *was* bad luck."

Andy nodded sadly.

"You still want to stay straight, though? You think if you got away from this house you could?"

"I think so. Yeah. I was doing okay until this."

"Well look, I had a place arranged and then a friend talked me into staying somewhere else. It might still be available. It's a room in a halfway house for people being released from jail. I know you'd qualify but I'd have to ask my PO if she could arrange it. Can you promise me you'll work the program while I look into it?"

"Where is it?"

"In Beaverton, out by The Round. Right near that central train and bus station."

"The Westside. Hell yeah. I can hang tough for that."

"I know you can," I said.

Andy tossed the cigarette butt into the pit, dug a pack of no-name cigarettes from the pocket of his jean jacket, and lit a fresh one. "You didn't come all the way out here to find me just to ask if I'm staying straight, did you?" he asked.

"Oh hell no. You aren't worth that much effort," I joked. "Actually, I need something. You hear about anyone ripping off a bunch of weed recently?"

Andy leaned back and looked at me, an expression I didn't recognize crossing his face. "Selling weed? I thought your thing was cage fighting and generally kicking ass. You in a new business these days?"

I had to smile. "No new business. Just looking into something for a friend."

"I hope she's pretty."

"Not as pretty as you, but yeah, she's okay."

"That's a relief. That you're not selling I mean. I want to stay away from all that shit, even weed, and you're the only person I met in jail I thought had it figured out."

"Ah, that's sweet. I'm like a role model."

We both laughed at that one.

"Seriously though, I need to figure out who burned a friend of mine."

"I wish I could help. Thing is I'm still new and with some of the house using, they're super paranoid. Dude, you and I know I wouldn't snitch anyone out for any reason, but they don't know that. They don't tell me shit. But tell me what happened, and where, and I'll do some digging."

"I don't want you digging too much. These guys might decide you really are a snitch."

"I'll be subtle."

"You don't know what that word means."

"Do too. Seen it on a bathroom wall once so I looked it up. That's how I got all my education."

"Looking things up?"

"Bathroom walls."

I groaned.

I was getting on the bike to head home when a phone rang. It took me a minute to realize it was *my* phone. I hadn't downloaded my old ring tone and the generic one didn't sound familiar. I finally fished it out of my pocket and caught it just in time.

"Hello."

"Hey, Bobby," said Howie. "It's me. You free to talk? Got some information for you."

"Great," I told him. "What did you find out?"

"Nothing you want to hear."

"Why? Is this guy that far out of my league?"

"So far out that you'd get a nosebleed just trying to find his address."

Howie knew I was a lightweight. After Jake and I aged out of foster care, we had no family to help us with college or a place to stay while we found work. The Sparrows were great, but they had other kids to raise. So, Jake and I got creative and experimented with a little criminality. Some of the people we'd met back then had stayed on that path. Howie was one of them, though only a player on the fringe. I'd gotten a little close to the fire—and a felony. It hadn't scared me straight, just into the Army. Jake had used college as his out. Only he never finished his second year. He wrote and sold, We All Fall Down, and his rebel without a pause main character made him rich enough and famous enough to drop out and write full-time.

"Letitia seemed to think he was just a low-level dealer," I said to Howie.

"The guy who ripped her off? I guess, well mid-level to be fair. From there it gets complicated."

"How?"

"Honestly I'm not sure."

"What?"

"I mean, I'm not sure why Oliver told me to stay away from the whole thing. He said the guy who ripped your friend off was just the tip of a big iceberg and I should give you a warning. If you're smart, stay out of it."

"Sounds more like a dare than a warning," I said. The smart ass retort out of my mouth before I could think. I realized my temper wasn't as controlled as I'd thought. So much for anger management classes.

"Don't be like that," Howie said. If Oliver says you should stay away it's not for nothing.

"That's all he told you? Warn your friend to stay out of it."

"I didn't say that. When I asked him if he knew who ripped off some marijuana, he told me who did it. But then he asked why I wanted to know, and I told him. When he realized I wasn't asking just to make conversation he got real serious. That's when he said I should tell you to stay out of it. He didn't say it like a threat, honest. It was more like I'd be doing you a favor."

From the moment Howie said, 'he told me who did it,' I pretty much quit listening.

"You have a name for me?" I asked.

Howie's sigh was so deep I heard it through the phone. He said, "Sure, but if anyone asks, it didn't come from me, right?"

"I know how it works," I told him.

"Okay then, the guy's name is Booker Robinson. He provides a lot of product, weed mostly, to the sports teams at the Center. Not the players, of course, they get tested, but their girlfriends and hangers-on. Other performers too. Rock stars. Country and Western singers."

"Letitia said he seemed legit."

"Yeah, I'd say so. He's been there for a long time. Works in events. Deals on the side. Everyone who's anyone knows, but he runs it clean and quiet. He's well-liked, and he isn't a user. From what I hear, even the events director is cool with him."

"Sounds like job security."

"Uh-huh."

"So why rip off the girls?"

"I thought you might ask me that. I have no idea. Sounds like an asshole move. Maybe it was too much money at one time for him to resist?"

"Maybe. That kind of makes sense. My friend says he was buying about three-quarters of a pound a month. That's a lot of weed but still only thirty thousand a year or so. At that rate, he wouldn't get rich."

"If that was his entire supply," said Howie. "And, if that was the only product he was selling."

"Yeah. Good point."

"You going after him?"

"Going to have a talk with him."

"I was afraid of that."

"Well, don't be. I'll be careful."

"No, you won't. You're Bobby Fucking Poe and you've never been careful a day in your damned life."

"I laughed. "This is why I like you, Howie. You know me and still talk to me."

"Yeah well . . ." he said, with no humor in his voice. "The people Oliver rubs elbows with sometimes scare me spitless."

"I will," I promised.

We both knew I was full of shit.

CHAPTER SIX

Finding Booker Robinson, once I knew his name and where he worked, was about as hard as finding Howie had been. This detective thing was way easier than it looked in the movies. First thing Monday morning I got on my phone and looked up the Moda Center, Portland's sports arena. They were kind enough to list their staff and for some of them, including Event Manager Booker Robinson, a photograph.

Ha, I thought. Got you.

Robinson was a middle-aged black man with a shaved head and a short beard and mustache that were turning gray. He wore narrow glasses. Maybe readers? Smiling at the camera, he seemed relaxed. His clothes were casual. A brown sweatshirt with the thin crescent edge of a white t-shirt peeking out. Only people who worked at Nike or other sports-based corporations could get away with dressing like a jock on their employer's website.

After that, it took two phone calls. First to get his number. "No thanks, I didn't want to be transferred," I told the person who answered the Moda Center's main number. I did want the number to Mr. Robinson, please. Once I had it, I made a direct call to his office, where once again, a receptionist or assistant type person answered.

"Hi, It's Dave Lombardo. I've got a one o'clock with Mr. Robinson but I'm running late. Could you let him know?"

"I'm sorry. What did you say your name was again?"

"Lombardo, Dave. I was sure a heavy metal drummer like Dave Lombardo wouldn't mind me, a fan, using his name for a good cause. Besides, he'd never know.

In a moment she came back with, "I'm sorry Mr. Lombardo but Mr. Robinson doesn't have you on his schedule."

"Oh. Maybe we were supposed to meet somewhere for lunch. Do you show a restaurant listed?"

"No sir, Mr. Robinson is booked in meetings until he leaves at five."

"I see."

"Would you like me to check other dates this week, in case he's made an entry mistake?"

"No, that's okay. I have to leave town tonight so it's now or never. It's too bad. He was so excited about booking the group. Tell him I'm sorry we couldn't make it happen."

"Well, I'm not really supposed to do this but let me see if I can connect you to his personal phone. Maybe he could fit you in."

"Thank you," I said. Trying not to sound too eager. I was, after all, a hardball businessman.

The phone rang three times and then a deep clipped voice said, "This is Booker Robinson. How can I help you?"

"Mr. Robinson. This is Dave Lombardo."

"The drummer?"

That threw me. I hadn't expected a Slayer fan. "Uh-um, no. I get that all the time. Same name. Different uh person."

"Gwen tells me you thought we had an appointment today?" He made it a question. He sounded like he was in a hurry and wanted to deal with me fast.

"Yes, we were supposed to meet to talk about a hundred bags of equipment that went missing." I let that sink in, then said. "What do you say we meet somewhere? We have a lot to talk about."

During the long pause, I could almost see the anxious thoughts racing through Robinson's mind.

"I believe we do," he finally said, and I knew his next words were for the benefit of someone there who could hear him. "Gwen says you thought we might have lunch together. If that works for you, I can be available for a late lunch, say one thirty?"

"That's perfect. Where do you want to meet?"

"Oh, somewhere close. Do you know O'Hallorans?"

It must be my week for Irish restaurants I thought. "Yes, I know it."

"Great. I'll meet you there at one thirty." Then he hung up.

I headed straight for the Moda Center and found parking for staff was beautifully marked. One thing I had to say about the Center, they did love to make their staff real and reachable, just like the ads said.

I parked in one of the handy visitor spots near the double doors at the back, grabbed a bottle of water out of a saddle bag, and took a seat on one of the benches flanking the doors. It was a warm day, and the sun was heating the black metal bench. Not too hot yet but it would be. I wasn't worried. I didn't expect to wait long, and I was right.

Robinson pushed through the doors, and walked past, oblivious to my presence. No slacker in the speed department, he headed with long strides toward his car… I left the bottle of water on the bench and hurried after him. About three steps from the black Lexus he was heading toward, he heard my footsteps. Should have got those Addidas. He started to turn, and I pulled the Glock from its holster, let him see it, then said, "Unlock the doors."

He pressed the fob twice and the locks on all four doors slid up, smooth as silk. "Toss the keys," I said, lifting my chin to indicate a parking lot island. He wasn't happy about it but tossed them away underhand. I heard them land in the brush but didn't see them fall. I wasn't going to look away from him. I wouldn't take bets on which of us would win in a fight. The gun was my only advantage.

"Dave Lombardo?" he asked.

"Get in and put on the seat belt, then put your hands on the top of the wheel," I told him. As soon as he'd done as I asked, I opened the back door, got in, and then shut the door by reaching across with my left hand. It had taken less than a minute. "Don't do anything stupid. I just want to talk." I slid across the seat until I could see between the front seats and be sure his hands stayed where they belonged.

"If you move, I'm going to shoot you. Do you believe me?"

He nodded.

One other thing I'd learned in the military—if you want to sound convincing—don't lie. I hoped I wouldn't have to shoot him, but I hadn't lied.

“How’d you know I’d take off?” he asked.

“Didn’t ask how you’d recognize me at O’Halloran’s. Also, you don’t look stupid.”

“Thanks. I’d guess you’re here to get the weed back.”

“You’d guess right.”

“Don’t have it.”

“You didn’t get rid of it that quick.”

“Well,” He hesitated a moment and I didn’t like that. “Not all, but a lot.”

“How much is left?”

“Half.”

“Who has the other half?”

“Bookie.”

“You’re a gambler?”

“Uh-huh.”

I sat with that for a moment. Howie told me Robinson was well respected. That he’d been working and dealing as a side gig for a long time. So, what he was saying didn’t ring true. Did it matter? Maybe not. The job was to recover Letitia’s stolen product. Half was a good start.

“You have it stashed where you can get it easily.”

"Yes."

"Where?"

He hesitated and I lifted the muzzle of the gun a little. "You think I won't kill you for fifty thousand? I know people who would do it for fifty bucks. You're a gambler. You want to bet on what my price is?"

I hoped he'd answer soon. I was starting to sound like one of those old-time gangsters in the black-and-white movies. Any minute I'd develop a Brooklyn accent and a sneer.

"My house. I got it locked up at my house. You can have it. I won't put up a fight. I paid off my debt. Don't need the rest anyway."

"Good of you," I said sarcastically.

My next decision was, who was going to retrieve the keys I'd had him toss away?

I decided he would. I tucked the gun away just in case there were parking lot cameras, or someone came out but kept my hand on it. I got out and opened his door, then told him to take off the seatbelt and get the keys. I stepped on the impulse to say, 'and no funny business.'

As he stepped out of the car, I backed away, staying far enough from him that he couldn't try some snaky move, like a leg sweep, or some other karate shit.

Once we were back in the car, with him in the driver's seat and me behind him, I pushed the muzzle of the gun into the fabric of his seat. Even a Lexus seat isn't that thick. He felt it and knew what it was.

"Go," I said.

CHAPTER SEVEN

Robinson lived in Laurelhurst, a neighborhood of older homes where the starting price tags were around a million dollars. I knew this because Jake had checked the area out before deciding on a house with a bigger lot and fewer neighbors. Again, I was puzzled. If the guy was living this well, why risk it all gambling and ripping off a supplier? It was a puzzle all right, but none of my business. All I wanted was to recover what I could and get it back to Letitia. I wasn't even sure if her fifty percent finder's fee still applied if I only brought back half.

The house was two stories with gables and stone steps going up from the sidewalk. The only parking was on the street. The driveway leading to a tiny one-car garage was so narrow I couldn't imagine even a

Mini Cooper getting into it. I would have liked pulling into a garage and a lot fewer eyes. Half a block away a group of teenagers were shooting hoops. Someone close by was running a lawn mower and cars rolled by steadily. I got out and looked around. "Come on," I told him. I had the gun in my hand pressed against my stomach under my jacket. Not obvious at all, I thought, mocking myself.

He got out of the car slowly and carefully then stomped up the stairs to the porch. The keys jangled in his hand. As he reached the door, he held them up. "Have to unlock," he said.

"Do it," I said.

He fumbled a bit and I readied myself. I expected him to drop, maybe throw the keys at me, distract me long enough to get inside. It's what I'd have tried. "Don't do it," I warned him.

"I wasn't going to do anything," he said, and maybe he wasn't. His churlish tone made me think he was annoyed by the unjust accusation.

"Good. Give me what I came for. You'll be fine and I'll be gone."

"Suits me," he said.

He walked in and I waited until he was standing in the middle of the wide living room before I followed. A gun's greatest advantage is that it can hurt or kill from a distance. Closing that distance reduces that advantage and introduces too many variables. Something I'd learned from a badass hand-to-hand combat instructor who also happened to be a trained sniper.

I stepped into the room, and someone slammed into me from the left. As I started to fall, my brain scrambling with surprise, my body responded instinctively. My left hand caught something, fabric, a sleeve. I used it as an axis to spin back toward whoever had smashed into me. Fighting to keep my balance and stay on my feet, I managed to get in close. So close that my hand holding the gun was jammed between us. That was okay, guns were never my thing. My thing was the ability to go from nice to murderous in a heartbeat.

I spun to my right, using my grip on the sleeve around his left wrist to pull him past me. Then twisted, so that my hip drove into his leg. I was hoping this, and his momentum, would make him lose his balance and fall.

He was tall, and skinny, all flailing arms and feet. The toe of one of his shoes caught my ankle. I almost headbutted the little asshole but I'd seen him up close. He was just a kid, and he was going down, falling to his knees. It hadn't been the best throw I'd ever done but it was good enough. As he lost balance, one of his windmilling arms knocked the gun out of my hand. I heard it skitter across the hardwood floor and looked up in time to see Robinson drop on it like Warren Moon on a fumble. There was only one thing I could do. I dropped behind the kid and put him in a stranglehold, pulling his head back and turning him to face Robinson, his body a human shield.

"Put the gun down," I barked.

"I don't think so," Robinson snapped back with the authority of a man with a gun.

"Drop it or—"

"Or what? You gonna snap his neck? That's for the movies."

"No, I'm not going to snap his neck. I'm gonna keep the pressure on his carotid. You see his face. He look okay to you?" I could feel the kid going slack, he'd fought at first, but a sleeper hold done right can knock someone out pretty quick. He slapped weakly at my hand. "Look, he's trying to tap out. Wrestled, didn't he?"

"What are you doing to him?"

"You know what I'm doing."

"Stop it. Please stop. I lied. I didn't make the payoff yet. I still have it. All of it."

"I don't believe you. Every time you open your mouth you lie."

"Not this time. Not about this. Stop or I'll blow your head off."

I dropped lower, so I was peering over the kid's shoulder, my head right beside his. "You better hope you don't miss. He's out now. His brain is starving. Much longer and he'll have brain damage. That what you want for this kid?" I was gasping, panting. Not just from exhaustion but from adrenaline overload. The kid's attack had been a shock. "Maybe you don't care about him," I said. "Maybe he just mows the lawn."

"He's my son," Robinson admitted. His voice was so shaky and fearful that for a moment I almost forgot I was a murderous son of a bitch.

"Take the gun by the muzzle and bring it to me," I commanded.

The kid made a snoring noise.

"Lungs are starting to shut down. He's going quick," I lied.

Robinson turned the gun around, doing as I said, and carried it to me, grip first. I kept my right arm around the kid's neck, my left forearm against the back of his head. His chin was down but he was breathing okay. I turned my palm up. Robinson put the gun in my hand. I wrapped my fingers around it and loosened my hold on the kid.

Robinson was backing across the room, hands up, palms toward me. "You let him go," he said. His voice was still shaking.

"Already did." I pushed the kid off me. He rolled to his side like a lanky sack of potatoes. Good looking kid. Looked like his dad. Thinner. Taller maybe. Black hoodie, Lewis & Clark Pioneers t-shirt, sweats, nice

Nikes. College kid. Eighteen or nineteen. Athlete. Solid prospects I'd bet. I got to my feet.

"I need to go to my son," Robinson told me.

I took a couple of steps back, then nodded. He rushed across the room, sat on the floor, and dragged his son's head into his lap. The kid was already waking up, mumbling, thrashing around a little.

"It's okay, Nathan. It's okay, son." his father told him.

The kid, Nathan, settled down a moment, then struggled to sit up.

"Stay there," I told them. I had crossed to where Robinson had been standing. "Get up and sit on the couch." They did so slowly and carefully. The fight had left them. For the moment.

I pulled my phone out one-handed and thumbed redial. Jake answered. "I've run into a little snag," I told him. "Can you meet me at an address in Laurelhurst right now? Yeah, it has to do with the Letitia thing. Sure, bring her along." I gave him the address, then hung up. I was holding two people at gunpoint and had figured it might be a good time to call for backup.

The Robinsons were sitting on the couch as instructed and speaking softly to each other. I didn't tell them to shut up. I didn't care what they were saying. I was pretty sure Robinson wouldn't do anything to put his kid in harm's way. A potential problem was the kid. He was young, and from the dirty looks he was shooting me, not too far away from trying me again. Still, I was pretty sure that his father would keep him in line.

All I wanted was to get Letitia's property back with the least difficulty. I knew the easiest way to do that was to have Jake go with Robinson while I held his kid. Jake wouldn't love it, but he'd see the necessity and play along.

"He might have a headache later," I said after about fifteen minutes had gone by.

"What?" Robinson asked.

"When you get the oxygen to your brain cut off like that. Sometimes you get a headache," I explained. "Could be in an hour, could be tomorrow. Maybe he'll get lucky and not get one at all. Just want you to know it's normal. It'll pass. No harm."

"No harm?" Robinson's eyes flashed fire. "If something happens to him. Anything—"

"Spare me," I said. "If you didn't want to put your kid in danger you shouldn't have gambled and you sure as hell shouldn't have ripped someone off. You're the one who put him in this situation."

"Gambled?" Dad, what's he talking about?" Nathan asked.

"Don't worry about it. This doesn't concern you."

"The hell it doesn't. What did you do?" When his father looked away and didn't answer the kid turned to me. "What did he tell you?" he asked.

I just shook my head.

"When your friends get here, you won't . . . you won't do anything to him will you?" the kid asked.

Jesus, could I feel more like a dick? "Nobody is going to get hurt if you stay calm and cooperate. Your father ripped someone off. They want their stuff back, that's all. They get it back; this will be over."

"You stole something to pay off my debt, didn't you?" Nathan Robinson asked his father. A small lightbulb lit up somewhere in my prefrontal cortex and I had a thought. Maybe the gambler wasn't Booker

Robinson. Maybe it was Nathan. Wow. Sometimes my quick grasp of complex situations is impressive.

CHAPTER EIGHT

Hyper alert, I heard footsteps on the porch and then a light rap on the door. "Don't move," I cautioned the two Robinsons. I stepped up to the window and moved the curtain aside enough to see it was Jake. "Come in and go to the right," I said loudly.

Jake opened the door, saw the two sitting on the couch on the left side of the room, and did as I'd asked, moving toward me and staying out of the line of fire. Letitia was right behind him, and Jake gestured for her to stay close. They moved up beside me. Jake was wearing a leather car coat. Warm for the weather. He reached inside it and pulled out a sawed-off shotgun. "I brought Bella Bang Bang, just in case."

"Good. Hopefully, you won't need her."

"She'll be terribly disappointed."

"She'll get over it," I gave Jake a smile I was sure made me appear even crazier to my captives. Then I looked at Letitia. "This the guy?

She nodded. "Yeah, that's him. "What the fuck were you thinking? she asked the senior Robinson. "Why would you rip me off? We ain't fucking thugs. We ain't dirty street. What the hell, man? I thought you were smarter than that. Marty vouched for you. Said you were smart. That you understood how to keep things quiet, and professional. This is a service industry, not the fucking mafia." With each word she seemed to be getting angrier.

"Calm down," Jake said.

That was a mistake. She turned on him instead. "Calm down? That what you tell Bobby, or is that just for the girls? Calm down. Be a good girl. Go to hell, Jake."

"Damn. I didn't mean it like that. I know you're pissed. You got every reason. I just don't want to have to mop up the blood after you lose your shit is all."

Letitia's scowl became her usual wry smile. "Goddamnit. You always did know the right thing to say. What do we know?" This time she turned to me when she spoke.

"I need to go somewhere and have a conversation with you. Jake, you keep these two here?"

Jake looked around. To the left, as you entered was a living area with a couch, an overstuffed chair, and a raw-edged coffee table. To the right was a dining room with a long table and six chairs. Jake took a dining room chair, pulled it away from the table, and turned it to face the couch. Then he laid the shotgun on the table, took off his jacket, and hung it across the back of the chair. Finally, he sat down, resting the shotgun across his lap. "There," he said. "Nice and comfy. You two can take your time."

I gestured at Letitia, and she followed me through the dining room through a kitchen and down a hallway lined with floor-to-ceiling shelves filled with books. The first room we came to was a small, neatly furnished bedroom that looked unused. Guest room was my guess. I closed the door softly.

"What's going on?" Letitia asked.

"That guy out there, his name is Booker Robinson. What they told you about him is true. He works at the

Center and deals to the players, sports people, at concerts, whatever. He told me he got in deep with gambling and had to rip you off to pay off the debt."

"Son of a bitch. I was going to use some of that money and take some time off. I wanted to take Tilly to Belize for the winter. You don't know this but I'm damn cheap and I never take her anywhere. Shit."

"Uh, yeah I do know that," I told her. "You have always been tight with money. Belize, for the whole winter? Guess you two are serious, huh?"

"You still hurt that I dropped you back then?" she asked.

"You didn't drop me." I protested. "I thought it was mutual."

"Whatever you want to believe. I saw how you were with Zoey. Everyone did. I'm not built to play second string."

I had no reply to that.

"Anyway," she continued, "Is this really the right time and place to discuss our love lives? Jake's holding a shotgun on two people."

"Right," I said, snapping back to the here and now. "Here's the thing. I thought this was just your normal simple greedy rip-off. I'd find the guy—"

"Which you did."

"Which I did. Only I don't think there's anything normal or simple about this. What I think is going on is that the kid got in trouble and dad ripped you off to save him. He didn't do it out of greed like I thought. He did it for his kid. You see the problem?"

Letitia let out a long sigh and put her hands on her hips. "The only problem I see is you."

"Come on. I know you better. If you take your stuff back that kid is going to be in deep shit with some bad people."

"Jesus, Bobby. I'm not a fucking monster but neither am I a saint. I can't let this lie. It would get around. Everyone would think I'm an easy target. Besides, I have expenses, bills to pay, a payroll. The guy stole from me, and you want me to just forget it, even help him?"

"I know it sounds crazy, but can't we at least talk about it? If you'd seen the way he was when I put a stranglehold on his kid. He was a quarter inch from pulling the trigger on me. He says he owes fifty thousand. I've been thinking about it. What if you let him keep half and I drop the finder's fee? You'll come out the same."

Letitia turned and sat on the edge of the bed. "You know what, Bobby Fucking Poe, you drive me crazy. You drive everyone crazy."

"That's been said," I agreed. "Will you talk to him? Would you try to find out what's really going on and if his story is legit, would you at least consider it?"

"Well sure, baby, but only because that's what all hardcore dealers do. We talk. We negotiate. We help."

"You did say it was a service industry."

"Fuck you."

Back in the front room, nothing had changed except the kid looked squirmier.

"I think Junior has to take a piss," Jake told me.

Well, that explained some of the restlessness. I pulled the Glock and gestured for Nathan to get up. "I'll take you to the restroom. My friend will watch your dad. You guys talk while I'm gone, okay?" I suggested looking at Letitia. She rolled her eyes but then nodded.

As soon as I got the kid alone I said without preamble, "You're the one with the gambling problem. What do you bet on?" I was leaning on the open doorway.

"Do you mind?" he said as if he expected me to close the door and give him privacy.

"Not at all. You go right ahead and take a piss. And while you do, you can answer my question."

"Fine," he said, turning his back as defiantly as someone in his situation could. "Sports. Okay. I bet on sports.".

"Huh, I had a friend made ten thousand dollars doing that," I told him. "Of course, she's smart and lucky. I'm guessing you're neither."

"Guess not," he said, zipping up and moving to the sink to wash and dry his hands. At least the kid had good hygiene.

"How much do you owe?"

For the first time, he looked seriously scared. "F-fifty thousand. It was only fifteen at first but when I couldn't pay…"

"Interest," I said, showing off my sage wisdom. Even so, that was an incredible amount.

"He told me to throw a game and we'd be even."

Ah, I was beginning to see the light. This was never about a fifteen-thousand-dollar debt. This was about putting a talented kid in someone's pocket.

"What game? Where?" I asked.

"I play basketball for Lewis & Clark." Unconsciously he looked down at the logo on his shirt.

"And they wanted you to make sure they lost a particular game," I offered. "I thought that was hard to pull off."

"Not if you're the center and the top point scorer. All I had to do was flub enough shots and the other team, they were good, they'd get ahead of us."

"But they didn't."

"I got nervous. There was a guy there, sitting right up front like he knew the coach or manager or something. I'd seen him before, just hanging around, and was pretty sure he was one of *his* guys. I got so nervous I fouled out. They put in someone else."

"He didn't flub?"

"Nope. We won. The next day the guy called me and said I owed him fifty thousand. He said if I didn't pay, he'd send some people to hurt my family."

"That fits with what your dad told me. Part of his story anyway. It keeps changing."

"It's not his fault. The guy I owe, he's bad, scary bad."

"Just who is this guy?" I asked.

"Mitch Miller," the kid told me, with the unhesitant honesty of someone who had not grown up with criminals or absorbed the childhood rhyme, "Snitches get stitches. "He's a bookie but he also sells steroids to some of the guys. They say he can hook you up with other stuff too, drugs, dates, whatever. They say he's connected to like organized crime or something."

After I got the kid settled back on the couch, me and Letitia took another trip to the guest room, and I told her most of what Nathan had shared.

"This is connected to like, organized crime or something," I said, mimicking the kid. "If he's right this is not good."

She rolled her eyes. "You think?"

I ignored the jab and said, "Well, the kid's story and the dad's match up pretty well. The kid got into debt. Dad could have probably paid that off, but the kid tried to fix it himself. Only he screwed that up and the debt got much bigger. Way bigger. Big enough that they were probably sure he had no way out. I doubt Robinson could scratch up that much cash. He has a nice house and car but he's probably carrying a mortgage and a car loan. Having to come up with that much money would have made him feel desperate. You must have looked like his only option."

"Yeah, but Bobby, you keep acting like this guy's some sort of superhero dad figure. Are you forgetting he's also a fucking drug dealer?"

My lips twisted. Even they weren't happy with what I was about to say. "So are you, hon."

Letitia had been facing me, her arms crossed. Now she uncrossed them and punched me on the shoulder. "You're such a dick." She took a deep breath and I saw her shoulders drop and knew she was giving in. "Fine. He can have half. We'll discuss the finder's fee."

I rubbed my arm. Those bony knuckles hurt. "You're awesome."

"I'm a moron."

In the living room, the Robinsons and Jake were talking about basketball. Jake was ripping on some Duck's player, and I was happy our appearance shut down the conversation. First, I hated sports talk, and second, Jake was supposed to be a scary bad man holding a shotgun. He was blowing his image.

"We talked," I said, nodding toward Letitia. "She feels that—"

"She feels," Letitia broke in and spoke directly to Robinson, "that she's going to take over your debt. I'm gonna let you have the weed you used to pay off your bookie, but you'll consider it a loan and we'll discuss a payment plan later. Now, let's go get my stuff."

I nodded at Robinson, and he said, "It's in the basement."

"Go ahead," I told him. He got up and his son followed.

At the basement door, I moved past and went down first. Robinson and his son were next, followed by Jake with the shotgun, and finally, Letitia.

The basement wasn't the dark hole of cobwebs and dirt I'd expected. Instead, it was finished and furnished as an entertainment space. A huge flat-screen television took up one wall. Beneath it, a long low set of shelves held DVDs and a couple of game systems. Four recliners were arranged in a single row, facing the screen. At odds with the rest of the tidy room, about half a dozen cork coasters, an ashtray, and the stubs of a few crushed cigars were strewn across the beige carpet. They had fallen from what had probably served as a coffee table. It consisted of two footlockers painted drab army green with a slab of raw-edged wood laid across them. The slab of wood had been pushed off and now leaned against one of the chairs. Both footlockers were open and empty.

"It's gone," Robinson said. He knelt and ran his hands inside one of the boxes as if he needed more than one sense to tell him the truth. He looked up at me and said, "I had divided it between the boxes because there was too much for one. That's why I told you I already paid off the debt. I thought maybe you'd believe me and not look in the other box. That would leave the rest and I'd be able to pay him off. But it's gone. It's all gone."

He sank down on the thick brown shag and rubbed his hands across his face.

“Who knew you had it?” Letitia asked.

“Just the bookie. He’s the only one I told. He called to warn me I was running out of time. Like a fool, I told him I was the one who burned you. Everyone had heard about it. I wanted him to know it had been me and I was good for Nathan’s debt. I told him, and I quote, ‘Don’t worry. I got it. It’s locked up safe and dry in my basement right now.’ The only thing I could have done to make it easier was give him the house key.”

“But Dad. He didn’t have a key, so how did he get in?” his son asked. “The front door is fine.”

Robinson leaned forward and rubbed his hands across his face, showing way more patience than I would have but then I don’t have any kids.

“Is it? How much do you want to bet the back door isn’t? You know, the one you can’t see from the street that has those handy panes of glass.”

“Oh, man. I’m so dumb.”

“Well, if you are you got it from me. I’m the one who told Mitchell where the weed was. He didn't even have to mess the place up looking for it. I was so anxious to make sure you were safe I never thought . . . Goddamnit, they got double what you owed them."

"Maybe, but that don't mean they get to keep it," Letitia snapped. "Who is this fucking bookie?"

I have to admit, her anger was better than listening to Booker beat himself up.

"Mitch Miller," Nathan said, answering for his father.

"Oh shit," Letitia said.

Her defeated tone got me and Jake's attention. Jake raised an eyebrow.

"Mitch Miller," she explained, her brow wrinkled like she was puzzled we didn't get it. "You don't know who he is? He works for Hugh Rose."

Hugh Rose. Psycho brother of Oliver Rose, Howie's boss. Great.

"Well, we are well and truly screwed," said Letitia.

Nathan spoke first. He was the only one young and dumb enough to voice what none of us would.

"Why don't we take it back?"

His father, who was still sitting on the floor looking abjectly miserable, looked up at his son with disbelief. "No more ideas from you. Not today. Maybe not for a long time."

"But she said . . ." Nathan nodded toward Letitia.

"That was before we knew who we were dealing with," Booker told his son.

"But why can't we?" asked Jake.

Now it was time for all of us to turn our attention to him. We stared, but no one said a word.

"Bad idea?" he said.

"Ridiculous idea," said Letitia. "I'd never let you do something so stupid. After all, it's just money."

If the Robinsons hadn't been there, I'd have no doubt said something clever, like, 'Has anyone seen Letitia?' but they were there so I kept quiet. Of course, she was right.

Robinson got to his feet. "I need a drink. Anyone else?"

"I sure as hell do," said Jake. Slinging the shotgun over his shoulder he headed toward the stairs. We all followed him up. When we reached the kitchen, Robinson opened a cabinet and took out a new bottle of Four Roses bourbon. What else. Irony is a nasty kind of humor.

He put it on the counter and turned back to the cabinet for glasses. I picked it up and tried to twist off the cap but it resisted. The machine that cut the scores had botched the job. It would need a little help. Not thinking, I reached over my shoulder and under my jacket collar where I'd long ago sewn a leather sheath that housed a knife with a thin blade. I pulled it out and slipped the tip under the seal and cut the cap free. It had become very quiet, and I looked up to find everyone staring at me.

"What?" I asked.

"You have that the whole time?" Robinson asked.

"Sure."

"Why didn't you use it? Why didn't you pull it on Nathan?"

I looked at the blade in my hand. "I wasn't going to kill him, Robinson. He's just a kid."

"Call me Booker," he said. Then he handed me a tumbler.

It was kind of unreal to sit in the living room of the man I'd abducted and sip his bourbon. I had the gun holstered and clipped to the front of my jeans. Booker and Nathan were side-by-side on one end of the couch. Letitia was on the other end, nearest the door. I had taken the big armchair while Jake had pulled up the dining room chair. The shotgun was lying sideways across his lap, and he was leaning forward casually, one elbow resting on the stock. It was almost as if he'd forgotten it was there or what its purpose was. He hadn't. No one had.

"Don't suppose it would do any good to suggest to Mr. Miller that he took more than he was owed," said Letitia.

"Been thinking about that," said Jake. "Would it cause any trouble if we told Miller's boss? I mean was he supposed to do that? Isn't it sort of like ripping off the boss to take twice what's owed and keep half for yourself?"

"If he did that. How do we know he didn't turn it all over?" asked Letitia. "Even if he didn't, you want to bet that his boss would fail him for showing initiative? He got the job done, after all. He delivered enough product to cover the debt. Anything over would be frosting."

"Yeah, but maybe the boss would like a lick of that frosting," said Jake.

"That makes sense," agreed Booker. Plus, even if the boss doesn't want the extra—frosting—
as you call it, he still might not like being kept in the dark."

As they argued the finer points of keeping secrets from Hugh Rose, I took long sips of my drink, sucking air through my teeth to wake the flavor. It was smooth and warm, everything I wanted in a bourbon. As good as the stuff Howie had bought when we were at Murphy's. Maybe not but hard to say. I'd need to sample more.

I didn't bother getting involved in the conversation. I already knew the outcome. Nathan might not understand the cost of being known as a snitch in certain circles, but I certainly did and so did Jake, Letitia, and Booker. None of us were innocent kids. None were adults who didn't understand the consequences of doing that. At least within the subculture of criminality we had involved ourselves in.

Letitia and the Robinsons would toss ideas around for a while. They'd vent some frustration and eventually land right where we were, recognizing who we were. People who weren't playing by the rules and who therefore didn't get to call in the rule keepers.

Letitia and Booker had lost. The kid had, maybe, learned a valuable lesson. Life would go on and damn, this was some good bourbon.

Since I'd more or less hitched a ride with Booker, I had to hitch another with Jake in order to get my bike. Letitia made me sit in the back seat, of course. She was still pretty pissed. Who wouldn't be? That was a lot of money and anger to leave behind. I think she'd have been happier if I'd come back to her with a story of losing the money but kicking Booker's ass.

Unfortunately, she'd met him and heard his story so now had all the same complications running around in her head that I did. It was no longer a matter of simply taking stuff from a bad guy. That made it much harder for her because now she had to readjust where she focused her anger at being ripped off. The bad news was, that I was handy and a convenient scapegoat. The good news was that my bike was right where I'd left it, just as I'd left it. Not even so much as a parking ticket.

CHAPTER NINE

Jake's publisher, or agent, or whoever it is that arranges those kinds of things, had booked him on a two-week tour of bookstores on the East Coast. As much as he liked to bitch about those, I think he was happy to leave Letitia's mess behind. He had probably thought it would be easy. Find the thief. Steal the stuff back. Make Letitia happy. Make me happy. Poor Jake, always trying to make everybody happy. It must wear him down.

While he was out of town, I decided to get busy and find work. I mean, actual nine-to-five, day-in and day-out work. My PO had "suggested" I register with the employment office, so I did. I'm nothing if not compliant. They had a few jobs listed for mechanics, two working at car dealerships, and another maintaining a fleet of golf carts. I also considered a job as a cook. I'd done a fair share of that on my cross-country trip.

Unfortunately, all of the jobs I found were entry-level with a probationary period before you got bumped up, so the pay was worth getting out of bed. I didn't want to wait that long. I needed decent money right out of the gate. That was the excuse I gave myself for not applying. The truth was none of them came close to the promise of that fifty-thousand-dollar payday I'd given up. I was feeling sorry for myself, wallowing in it, but it wouldn't last. In a few days, I'd be out of cash and my attitude would change. Hunger is a great motivator.

Whenever I wasn't reading ads or haunting the employment office I worked on the car. Not that I could do much. Without parts money, it was less build and more dismantle.

One afternoon I got Heather to run me to my unit at the storage place and we moved all my stuff into her SUV and then unloaded it at the duplex. I put everything in the bedroom closet and was even trying to figure out how to squeeze in a couple of tires when she stopped me.

"Aww, gross. You're not going to keep those stinky tires next to your clothes, are you?" she asked.

"Of course not," I said, pretending I was shocked by her accusation. Then, under her watchful eye, I carried them outside and locked them in the backseat of the car.

Once I'd quit acting like "such a guy," and was back in her good graces, she told me she wanted to set me up on a blind date with a friend of hers. "Megan is your type," she said and showed me a picture in her phone of a slender blond with a heart-shaped face. "She looks like Zoey, don't you think?"

"She does, a little," I said. "It's just right now I'm busy trying to get my life together. I don't have time to go out. Maybe in a few weeks."

"Can't promise she'll be available that long but check back with me," she said. I laughed because she sounded so much like the guy at the tire store the day before when I'd gone in to look at custom rims I couldn't afford.

"Better order them now," he'd said. "Not sure how long they'll be available." Dating was apparently not that much different than buying parts.

Heather stayed for dinner, and I made tacos, her favorite. After she left, I cleaned up the place and then sat down to stare at the television. I say stare because I wasn't really watching it. I was thinking of the picture Heather had shown me and thinking about all the ways Heather's friend was not Zoey.

Megan was pretty enough, and was a Zoey type, with long hair and big eyes, though Megan's were blue and Zoey's brown.

The thing is, Megan was beautiful, but Zoey had both beauty and charisma, a powerful combination. The world is full of beautiful women but more than once I've seen Zoey cross a room, go into a bar, or find a table in a restaurant with the same result. Every person in the place would eventually turn to look at her. Some even found excuses to come up and talk to her. I've had bartenders and waiters, hell waitresses for that matter, take her order and rush off to get what she wanted, never even asking for my order. It was as if they didn't see me, the suddenly invisible man.

When she was in a good mood she'd look around, focus those huge brown eyes on someone, and smile. All those watts of power directed at a mere human. It seemed to stun them, silence them. After whatever transaction that brought them into her aura was over, they'd linger nearby. It was like the energy she gave off filled some need of theirs. Zoey was magic. It's bad when the one who got away is magic. The world is a whole lot less after that.

Life, as they say, moves on, even if you don't notice that is has. I had an appointment with my probation officer on Monday. I'd written the appointment on the free calendar I got from the tire shop. I'd even circled it twice with a red Sharpie I'd found in the "junk" drawer in the kitchen. I was determined not to be a fuck up.

I got to the appointment early and hung around in the reception area waiting to be called back. Ten minutes past my appointment time, my PO came out and said my name. So much for getting there early. I pushed down the little bubble of annoyance. Ten minutes was nothing. Doctors made you wait longer, even if you were bleeding. I was just unhappy to be there, stuck in the same room with a lot of other losers. That wasn't her fault. Besides, I owed her for getting Andy into the halfway house in Beaverton. It would give him a better chance at recovery than the place he'd been staying.

Before this, I had only talked to her on the phone. She had dark red hair, no doubt dyed, and lipstick to match. Both things made her look older, which was probably the point. The freckles and general perkiness were harder to disguise, and she was a lot younger than I'd expected. She got right to business though. Pulled out my file. Ran one short nail down the page as she read me the rules.

The gist of the meeting was that if I stayed out of trouble for six months, I'd be free. No more supervision. I smiled and nodded, trying to decide if someone filled with visions of rehabilitation chirping in my ear was better than an old, burned-out civil servant. I finally decided it didn't matter. I was already hanging out with known felons and carrying weapons. Who my PO was wasn't the important thing, not getting caught was.

When I got home, I found Andy waiting for me. He was sitting on the single wide step that served as my front porch.

I parked the bike and he got to his feet. He looked good.

"Hope you haven't been here long," I said as I walked toward him.

"Nope. Not long."

"How'd you get here?"

"Took the bus. Bus stop's right there, dude."

He pointed up the block and I saw the familiar blue and white sign. Funny how I hadn't noticed it before. The blindness of privilege. If it weren't for Jake I'd also have to know the location of every nearby bus stop.

We went inside and I grabbed a couple of sodas out of the refrigerator. We sat and talked for a while, stories about things that happened in jail mostly because that's where we met. Neither of us really wanted to talk about that place though so the conversation quickly stalled. Finally, I asked if he wanted to give me a hand with the Coronet. "I pulled the engine and now I want to pull the transmission. Be easier with some help."

"No problem," he said. So that's how we spent the next couple of hours.

When we were done, we went in to clean up and I got us a couple more sodas. What I really wanted was a beer, but drinking a beer in front of Andy would be a shit thing to do. I felt bad enough that he got grease on his shirt while he was helping me. Borrowing from Heather's generosity, I gave him one of the shirts she bought me. He tried to refuse it of course, but I finally won, and he tucked it into his backpack.

"I already owe you," he said. "This house you hooked me up with is the real deal. These are serious guys really trying to work the program. Good people, dude. We have fun. Got a pool table in the garage. Dart board. We take turns cooking but everybody pitches in. We got one kid they call Preach. He does a reading from the bible on Sundays. You can go or not. I went this week. Probably going to keep going. Hell Bobby, I'm even gonna try to quit smoking. They got a program for that. Hook you up with gum, patches, whatever you need."

"That sounds like where you need to be," I said and believed it. This pulling yourself up by your bootstraps idea is bullshit. Some of these kids don't even have bootstraps. People need support. Most get it from their family but a lot of the kids I grew up with in the foster care system didn't have that. With no family to help and a system that kicks you out when you reach eighteen, ready or not, what would you expect? Some of those kids are damaged and angry. Some of them are vulnerable and easy prey. Others, like Heather, have learning problems or disabilities, and with no one to help them make good decisions, they can make really bad ones. A lot of them end up in prison and with a record the downward spiral is nearly assured.

Just thinking about it could make me start into a downward spiral of my own. At least Jake was trying to do something about it, keeping in touch with everyone, and helping when he could.

Andy hadn't been a foster kid, but he was the next thing to it. He told me he never knew his father and his mother died when he was barely out of his teens. If it weren't for his uncle helping him out now and then he'd have been living under a bridge. His voice pulled me out of my musings. He was still talking up his new place.

"Yeah, you're right. It is where I need to be. I fit in and they trust me. I asked if they heard about that rip-off, you told me about, remember?"

"Sure," I said, but I didn't offer more. I'd rather change the subject and not drag him in deeper by telling him what I'd learned. It didn't matter since it turned out he already knew almost everything I did.

"I found out the guy who stole your friend's stuff is a dealer," he told me. "Rumor is he did it to pay a debt he owed to Mitch Miller. Miller's one of Hugh Rose's crew. Him and this weird accountant guy run one of his clubs. I don't know how much Miller manages it though. He's more of an enforcer. The kind of guy who breaks your nose or your leg if the boss asks him to. His boss runs all kinds of gambling, from illegal sports betting to casino games in his clubs. I think he's into some other shady stuff too, but gambling is his big money maker. You've heard of Hugh Rose, haven't you?"

"Yeah, I've heard of him. He's the reason we decided to let it go."

"Let it go? That doesn't sound like you."

"What can I say? I'm getting older and wiser. Okay, older anyway."

"Well let go of letting it go. I know how your friend can get even."

"She doesn't want to get even," I told him. "She just wants her property back."

"That's what I mean. Balance the books. Only you know they don't still have her stuff, right? It would have gone to their street dealers by now or been sold to someone who could get rid of it."

"Exactly. That's another reason to let it go."

"Or you could take something of theirs of equal value."

"That sounds like a bad—"

"No. Listen. Hugh Rose collects sports memorabilia. He's known for it. Likes to show it off. He's got all this stuff, signed footballs, rookie cards, game shirts. You name it, dude. There's a rumor he's even got a Lebron James card worth over a million. I know you think I'm a loser addict but before I got into that shit, I had some mad skills. My uncle taught me. I told you about him before. You can look him up. He's so famous he's got his own Wikipedia page. He was a thief, and he could get into any house, open any safe."

"Where's this uncle now?" I asked, pretty sure the answer would be dead or in prison.

"Not sure. He's got a place in France because he likes skiing and a place in Belize because he likes the beaches. He's retired so we can't ask him to help, though I'm sure he'd give us advice."

It was surreal. An image of Andy's uncle flashed through my mind, a James Bond-looking character, stuffing his suit pockets with necklaces that dripped diamonds and emeralds, their facets sparkling as he stood at the window of a mansion, getting ready to climb out and escape. That picture in my mind would make a great movie poster or book cover.

Andy saw my expression and mistook it for interest.

"We grab a couple of those sports things. My uncle hooks us up with one of his buyers. Your friend covers her losses and man, you'd be a hero."

"A hero? You almost made me shoot this Mountain Dew out of my nose. That carbonation shit hurts. A hero?"

"What, you don't have the legs for tights?" Andy snorted, laughing at his own joke. "Come on, dude. Now that I'm straight I'm ready to get back to work. This job would be a good challenge for me."

"No, this job would be a good way to get your ass shot. It's not going to happen. Sometimes the smart thing is to walk away, like you had to walk away from where you were living. Sometimes there are better choices. Like my friend taking her losses, or you looking for a real job. When we met you were in jail, remember? Thought you were done with that."

"Done with drugs, yeah dude. Done with getting caught, for sure. Not done with making a living. What kind of regular job would someone like me qualify for? Nondescript and able to disappear in a crowd. Good with locks. Climbs like a spider. That's a pretty strange set of skills."

I thought about it a minute, thought about how Andy always acted dumber than he was. I had to keep that in mind when arguing with him. I said, "Locksmith leaps to mind. Multi-story window washer? Security expert?"

"Well hell. Those don't sound like fun."

"They call it work for a reason. Quit pouting. Any of those would still be more fun than jail."

"My uncle's not in jail," he reminded me smugly.

"Yeah, well you aren't your uncle, plus, times have changed. Everyone has security cameras and alarms now. Besides, what about the whole stealing stuff from someone who worked hard to get it thing? The thief is never the good guy. You want to be the bad guy?"

"Jesus Bobby. What's with the morality lecture? We're not talking about ripping off your grandmother. This is stealing from a criminal. Nothing wrong with that. Man, I didn't come here for a lecture. I came here to help you."

"I know. I get that," I told him. "I didn't mean to come off all righteous. I've done enough shady stuff in my time but like I said, we met in jail, and I don't think either of us want to end up back there."

"Yeah, well, I guess," he said, calming down.

"Will you at least think about looking for a regular job? My PO had me register with the employment office and they told me about this retraining program. Maybe you should check it out."

"Maybe."

"Good. You want a ride home? I've got an extra helmet."

It didn't take much urging. Sitting on a bike is always better than sitting on a bus.

When I got back storm clouds were gathering and the sky was getting dark. It would probably rain all night just like it had the night before. I was thinking about that as I pulled into the driveway and spotted Jake's car in the driveway next door and then Jake sitting on the front stoop.

As I walked up, I said, "Why have all my friends decided waiting around for me is better than, I don't know, texting, calling?"

"What are you talking about?" Jake asked.

"Found Andy sitting there earlier. He helped me work on Princess. Just getting back from running him home."

Princess huh? Thought you were changing the name."

"I will. Soon as I get rid of that pink pinstripe."

Jake saluted me by lifting the bottle of beer he was holding. "I just got back an hour ago. Didn't feel like unpacking so I drove over here instead."

"Why didn't you let yourself in," I asked, as I unlocked the door.

"Sure, and get sued by a pissed off tenant. No thanks. Got a beer out of my fridge and I don't know, kind of wandered over. What are you doing? You want to go and get something to eat?"

"Where's Cassandra?"

"Out. Some kind of girl's night out thing."

"Book club?"

"More like several lawyers getting shit faced."

"Ah. More fun than a book club."

"No doubt."

Jake got up and followed me inside.

"If you want another beer, you know where they are," I told him. "I've got to hit the john. Long ride. Cold wind."

When I came back, I saw Jake sitting slumped on the couch, Zoey's blanket draped across his legs. He'd opened a beer for me and set it on the coffee table. I sat down, grabbed it, and took a long swallow. Nice. I was about to brag about spending a whole beer-free day for the sake of Andy when I noticed Jake's hands were shaking.

"You cold?" I asked, nodding at the afghan.

"Yeah, a little."

Fuck. Maybe he was and maybe he wasn't but that wasn't why his hands were shaking. Jake didn't shake like a drunk coming off a three-day binge except when he was deep into using his drug of choice. That would be the CIA's favorite mind control drug, beloved by hippies and hipsters everywhere, lysergic acid diethylamide. Lot of people used LSD but Jake had elevated its use to a fine art. Last time he'd gotten heavily into it I'd postponed going into the service because I'd been so worried about him.

His drug use wasn't the only problem. It was more a symptom of the depression that came over him like one of those dark clouds above us. The two, depression and LSD, seemed linked but like the chicken and the egg, I was never sure which came first.

What if he'd been dropping acid on this book signing thing? Maybe it was a one-off. Something he played with while he was out of town. Now that he was back, he'd stop. These were the thoughts and explanations that whipped through my mind. No reason to panic. Not yet.

"How'd your trip go?" I asked, aware of the wordplay but not even slightly amused.

He shrugged and stared down at the carpet under his feet. "Okay," He hesitated a moment then said, "You ever feel like you aren't who everyone thinks you are?"

I sort of stumbled over the question. "Sure. I guess. I mean, is anyone who they seem to be? Where is this going?"

He shrugged again. "I don't know. Had this fan at one of the signings. Smart. Well read. Maybe early twenties. She'd read "Fostering Fear," the first one, the good one, you know?" He looked up and I could see undisguised pain on his face. "She asked me when I was going to write another book."

"You told her—"

"Yeah, I told her I had written eight more. She said, sure, and those were great thrillers. She understood that I had to make money with the more popular genre fiction, but was I working on something else? The subtext being anything worth a shit. I told her I was working on a special project and not to tell anyone. Said it was hush-hush. Fuck. I'm such a liar. Such a goddamn phony. I don't have a special project. No great American novel in the works. I'm just cranking out the same old shit day in, day out."

"What? Your books are great. You can't let one person—"

"Yes, I can. If that person is right. That first book. There was honesty there. I wrote about us, the kids we grew up with. The kids we were. I talked about the horror stories and the good times. I ripped open the belly of foster care and invited everyone to look inside. Now I just kill some innocent moron and then have my dimwit character run around trying to figure out who did it. I mean, how hard is that? I already know who did it. The only trick is keeping it a secret until the bitter end. What a joke."

I wanted to come back with how few people can pull off that trick, but he was far too deep into self-pity. Words weren't going to help. I realized, with a sick feeling, that my first instinct had been right. Jake was heading down the well, as he called it. Spiraling into that dark place where no one could follow. It explained him using again. Self-medicating but with the wrong medicine. Truth was he probably could use some chemical assistance, a prescription written by a doctor though, not a sheet of blotter.

"How long you been dropping acid?" I asked, and though I hadn't meant them to, the words sounded like a harsh accusation.

He sat back and glared at me. "As long as I fucking want."

"And exactly how long is, as long as I fucking want?" I asked, trying for humor and failing miserably.

His shoulders dropped and as he lost the aggressive stance he sighed. "I don't know. A little while. Just on weekends when Cassandra has to be out of town. I bought a little property out in Mist a year ago. A couple of acres with a house that needs to be pulled down but a decent barn. I got a tent set up in there. A solar heater. It's nice. Sort of a camping spot but with a roof to keep off the rain. I get out there. Drop a couple hits. Try to get my head in the right space to write something worthwhile. If I could reconnect with that creative place where "Fostering

Fear" came from I could do it again. I could find the words. I know they're out there somewhere."

"Or maybe they're in here," I said, pointing to my temple. You know those words didn't come from some laboratory. They came from your brain. You let some kid push your buttons."

"You wouldn't understand," he said, and he leaned forward and put his beer down with a thump.

"Yeah, you're right. I don't understand at all. You got money, fame, a great girlfriend, the house, the cars. Your life sucks."

"Like I said. You don't get it."

He got up and left, not even bothering to slam the door behind him.

CHAPTER TEN

After Jake took off I had a hard time getting to sleep and was still half worried and half pissed when I woke up the next morning. Coffee helped me realize I had better things to do than nurse a sad prima donna, even if he was my brother and best friend.

I was working in the carport when one of the neighbors, out on his morning run, stopped to admire the Coronet. We ended up talking cars and he told me he'd been saving to fix up the '57 Chevy sedan his grandfather left him. He needed help with the restoration, so we struck a deal and suddenly I had a job. Maybe not a nine-to-five, but at least it would give me a little breathing room. The neighbor, whose name was Henry, cut me a check that day. Some people are ridiculously trusting. In this case, being on the receiving end, I was okay with that.

Jake called that afternoon, apologized for the sudden exit the day before, and asked me to come to dinner on Friday. "Bring your friend, what's his name, Andy, with you," he suggested.

After we hung up, I considered why he'd asked me to invite Andy. Was it his usual sociable nature, or did he think a new face would serve as a buffer, a way to keep us on our best behavior? He didn't have to worry. I was done trying to lecture Jake about his use of hallucinogens. Like any addict, he was the only one who could decide when and if to get straight. I'd be around to help if he asked, otherwise, I planned to keep my mouth shut. Maybe the months in rehab while I was in jail had been time well spent.

I had learned stuff.

Dinner was good. Jake ran the grill, but it was Cassandra who ran the show. Rain was threatening so she'd set the big table in the kitchen, family style. There was a cold bucket of chicken from KFC, a tub each of deli-bought coleslaw, potato salad, and baked beans.

"You guys each take a platter and go get the steaks and corn that Jake's got on the grill, would you?" she asked.

We hurried to comply. I was starving and it was easy to see that Andy was awed by Jake's house and Cassandra's warm welcome.

"You cooking for an army?" I asked Jake when I saw the thick steaks and brats. The dripping fat sizzled and the smell made my mouth water.

Jake used tongs to lift off ears of corn, wrapped in their husks, and place them on a tray Andy held out. He said, "Heather is coming as soon as she can. Little Mikey said he'd try. Letitia and Tilly were going to pick up dessert but should be here soon, so the answer is yes, I *am* cooking for an army."

I felt the gentle pat of fat raindrops and looked up. The dark clouds were lower in the sky. "Those steaks ready?" I asked. "I think we're about to get rained on big time."

Jake put the last ear of corn on the platter and Andy headed back inside then Jake glanced at the sky.

"I think we'll make it. They're ready," he said and using the same tongs began loading brats onto my platter. On top of them, he laid three huge steaks. This done, he turned off the grill and we headed for the door at a quick jog. We almost made it, but the deluge caught us just as we reached the door. Jake flung it open, and we scrambled inside, skidding a little, both of us breathless and laughing. As I set the platter on the table, the front door opened, and a damp wind blew through the house.

Letitia came in with Tilly close behind. Water streamed from them both. They put three pink boxes on the counter, which I assumed held dessert, then Cassandra led them to the guest room where they could leave their coats and purses. I could hear them laughing and talking as I took it upon myself to cut the steak into reasonable portions. Andy was unwrapping and buttering corn. The kitchen was filled with the scents of good food, perfume, and weed. I looked around at my friends and realized I was humming. Zoey's absence caused a pang, but I put it aside and realized I was happy.

Before the girls returned to the kitchen there was a knock on the front door. Jake went to answer it and came back with Little Mikey. A minute later Mikey ran to the door to let Heather in. As the people I thought of as my family slowly arrived and found their places around the table, bitching about the weather and exclaiming about the amount of food I realized that pretty much everyone I gave a damn about was here, in this one room. For a moment I considered how quickly they could all be gone. The image of a plane crashing into the house suddenly flashed through my mind. I imagined a massive explosion and bodies flying everywhere. The image was graphic, and of course, ludicrous. I pushed it away and concentrated on the conversations going on around me.

Little Mikey and Andy were talking about a security system Mikey had just installed. That figured. Letitia and Tilly were sitting across from me. Tilly was talking to Cassandra about the best fertilizer for growing flowers. Something about chicken versus horse manure.

Letitia seemed to be ignoring this conversation, intent on cutting bits of steak, dipping them in horseradish sauce and chomping happily. She had apparently slipped out of her shoes, as I could feel her toes slowly working their way up my legs. I wagged a finger at her, and Tilly stopped eating long enough to give her partner a look and say, "For God's sake woman, will you leave that man's crotch alone?"

Everyone laughed but Letitia didn't stop, just smiled at me and wrapped her lips around another slice of steak. Naughty woman. Andy was the only one who looked a little uncomfortable. Poor guy didn't know this was the usual kind of thing that went on between us. He was probably considering the number of steak knives within Tilly's reach.

I grabbed Letitia's shapely foot to get her attention, and when I had it I said, "Just want you to know Andy is one of the people I went to for help about your situation with Miller."

"Oh," she said, withdrawing her foot, somewhat to my regret. "Nice to meet you," she said turning toward Andy. I guess I can say I appreciate you trying to help me. After all, everyone here knows about my situation." She drew air quotes around the word situation. "So, I suppose we can all talk openly about it.

There's something I was going to talk to you and Bobby about later but might as well go ahead if Andy's in on things."

"Oh," Jake said, and shot a pointed glance at Cassandra.

"Oh right. Sorry," said Letitia.

Cassandra shook her head but didn't say anything.

"I'm sorry, babe," Jake said to her.

There was a deep silence around the table and Letitia looked uncomfortable, but she was the first to speak. "This is my problem, Cass. I shouldn't have dragged Jake into it."

Cassandra scooted her chair back and got up. Her face revealed nothing, and I realized I'd never want to play poker with the woman. I think we expected her to leave the room and were all surprised when she went into the kitchen and started opening the boxes Letitia and Tilly had set on the counter.

"I see you guys brought the dessert like you promised. Three kinds of pie, that's nice. I was kind of in the mood for cake though. Chocolate cake. Sound good to anyone?"

No one responded to her rhetorical question.

"I'll be right back." She grabbed her raincoat and keys and left. A few minutes later we heard her car pulling away.

"I'm sorry about that," Leticia said to Jake. "Your lady, she's something though."

"She is," Jake agreed. "Now, what was it you wanted to talk to us about?"

"I got a call from Booker."

"Booker?" asked Andy.

"He's the guy who ripped her off," I explained. "Booker Robinson, the one who deals from the Moda Center."

Andy nodded and Letitia told him, "After he stole the weed from me, Miller stole it from him. Did you know about that?"

He nodded. "I heard Hugh Rose ended up with it."

"That's right. Your friend here," she gestured toward me, and long red nails had never looked more lethal. "Well, he has some old-fashioned, some might say archaic, ideas about things. For instance, he decided that the guy who ripped me off had such a good reason for doing it that we should pat him on the head and say, 'atta boy.'"

"I never said—"

"Hush you. Anyway, like I said, we let Booker go. Of course, I'm not the saint Bobby is. He has to pay me back. We even arranged a payment plan we could both live with. So, maybe I'm not a saint, but I am civilized."

"Uh-huh," I said without expression. Daring to interject anything was brave if I do say so myself.

She shot me a look from dark eyes then reached down and wrapped long fingers around her wine glass before saying, "He called me this morning. I thought it was to arrange the first payment. Nope. You know what he called to tell me? You want to guess?"

She looked from me to Jake and back again.

"I have no idea," said Jake.

"Well get ready to be surprised. It seems he has decided that I'm not just the supplier he ripped off, I'm a friend. Someone to call when bad things happen. He wanted to share with me that he got a call from Martin. Martin wanted to know when he was going to pay his debt."

"What?" Both Jake and I said at the same time.

"That son-of-a-bitch!" said Jake, catching on a second before I did.

"That's right," said Letitia. "He's pretending it wasn't his guy who stole the weed. He's going to hold Booker responsible for his son's original debt."

I said, "That fucker."

"That fucker, as you so aptly put it," said Letitia, "Is telling Booker that Nate has to throw the next game. He's going to ruin that kid's chance at getting on a team, and for what? First off, they added a ridiculous amount of interest, like I don't know the percentage." She looked at Tilly. "How much?"

"Seventy percent," Tilly supplied immediately, not looking up from scooping coleslaw onto her plate.

"Right. Seventy percent. So not only did they charge an outrageous amount on the original loan, but then they ripped him off for twice that. Now they don't want to credit him with it. I'm so mad I could cut a fucker." To make her point she let go of the wine glass and picked up a steak knife. "Who's with me?"

"With you on what?" Heather asked.

"On getting even with these assholes."

"What assholes are we talking about," Little Mikey asked. "I mean, from what I've heard there's a whole lot of them."

"That's right," said Heather. "We weren't part of the whole thing, but from what me and Mikey heard, there's a whole line of people who need . . . who need something."

"Like their asses whipped," said Little Mikey encouragingly.

"Right. Whose ass, or asses, are we going to whip, exactly?" she asked.

Jake and I exchanged a look. We both knew where this was heading, and we knew we could stop it if we wanted to. Unfortunately, as Andy had pointed out earlier, I wasn't good at dropping things. Neither was Jake. I recognized the look on his face. The raised eyebrow and crooked grin meant Jake was ready to go.

I couldn't help but smile back at him as I said, "Andy has an idea."

CHAPTER ELEVEN

Andy's idea of stealing Hugh Rose's sports collectibles got everyone's interest. It was Tilly who was first to say out loud what we were all thinking.

"The guy makes his money on sports betting so he can spend money on sports stuff. Taking it away is perfect justice for what he did to the Robinsons. I love it. Instant karma."

Little Mikey said, "I wonder what kind of security he has?"

"Hey, this is a me and Bobby thing," Jake told him. "You don't want to get involved in this."

"Oh, hell yeah I do," said Mikey. "I'm bored shitless lately. Helping you pull this off is going to be better than a weekend in Cancun. Andy's been telling me about his specialty. Between us, I figure we can get into any place you aim us at. Right, Andy?"

Andy nodded. "Yep, especially if we're talking about some kind of split. Hey, I've got bills to pay dude," he said, holding up his palms as if to show they were empty.

"You sure his collection is really worth that much?" I asked him. "It's just cards and signed balls and whatever, right?"

"Yep, just cards and whatever," he said, and rolled his eyes.

Andy and Mikey exchanged a glance that said without saying that I had a lot to learn.

"Couple of years ago a restaurant in Arizona was broken into," Andy said. "The thieves only took the sports memorabilia off the walls. When the insurance company came in they calculated the value of that old dust-covered stuff at over six hundred thousand dollars. A few weeks ago, someone stole a thirty-thousand-dollar card right off the table at a card show."

"How do you know all this," I asked.

"Google," he said. "You asked me to see what I could find out, dude. Once I started, I just kept going. Rose isn't hard to research. He uses his clubs and charities to get into the paper like some kind of celebrity. There's even a magazine article about his collection. Once I saw what he had, it wasn't hard to figure out the value."

Letitia got up and walked around the table, stopping behind Andy. I watched as she placed her hands on his shoulders, then slid them down his chest, ending up with her lips next to his ear. He had frozen in place, maybe afraid of the three-inch blood-red nails, more likely just afraid of that much woman. "You are my fucking hero," she said. Then she kissed his cheek. "My." Kiss. "Fucking." Kiss. "Hero." The last kiss was loud and enthusiastic. The rest of us cheered like kids.

Jake brought us back to reality. "Cassandra is going to be back any minute."

"We all agree that we're doing this?" I asked.

Everyone nodded. No surprise there.

"We need to do more research before we start planning the details," said Jake. "Little Mikey, how about you and Andy work on the security? Figure out the layout. Track down what Rose has and where he keeps it. Find out how we get in."

"And out," I added.

Jake nodded. "Yeah, don't forget an exit strategy. Letitia, how about you and Tilly talk to Andy about what pieces we should go for? We need to get your fifty thousand back and fifty for the Robinsons. One hundred thousand dollars is what we need to cover our losses. Andy, are you sure we can sell what we get?"

"Absolutely. Just remember we'll only get fifty percent of the real value so double up when you calculate what we take," he said, with a nod to Letitia.

"Okay, Bobby and me, we'll take turns and stake the place out. We'll see who comes and goes and figure out if there's a regular schedule."

"What about me?" asked Heather. "I want to do something."

No one spoke. Heather was someone we had always tried to help and protect. Whether that meant helping her study, doing her homework, or standing up against bullies. Putting her in any kind of bad situation was a no-go. I saw her expression change as she caught on.

"Jesus are you serious?" she asked. "I'm not a kid anymore. I don't need you to watch out for me. I'm also not a moron. I've got a learning disability, not a mental one. So, what if I can't read and math gives me a fucking headache. Give me any verbal test you want, and I'll pass. You all know that. Well, maybe not you Andy," she said, granting him a twisted smile before going back to glaring at each of us. "But the rest of you know I'm not dumb."

"No one thinks you're dumb," I said. "Honest Heather. It's just that Andy, Mikey, Jake, and me, well we have a little experience with B&E. You don't. We never thought of you as dumb. In fact, we always thought you were smart for not getting into the kind of shit we did."

She seemed somewhat appeased. At least her lips relaxed from a thin angry line and her fists unclenched.

"This is going to be more complicated than it sounds," I told her. "I'm sure we're going to need you somewhere. We just don't know where yet."

"Really?"

"Really."

"Getaway driver?"

"What?" said Jake.

"I kinda always wanted to drive a getaway car," she said, sounding deeply serious.

Jake and I exchanged looks.

Heather cracked up and soon we were all laughing. "You guys are so easy," she crowed.

"We all have our jobs," Jake said. We'll meet, well maybe not here, but somewhere, in a week to share what we learned. In the meanwhile, who wants pie?"

"Or some seriously good weed?" asked Tilly, setting an Altoid tin of bud on the table in front of her.

"Hey," said Letitia, unwrapping herself from Andy's neck. "Where's the music? Bring on the tunes. We're Ocean eleven, twelve and thirteening here. We need some kind of theme music."

"Hey, Bobby, what goes with we're gonna rip off the bad guy?" Heather asked.

I shook my head. "I will defer this decision to Jake. His house. His music."

Jake got up and went down the short hall to the living room.

"How about, "And Justice for All," by Metallica? he suggested.

"No More, No More, by Aerosmith?" offered Andy. Or maybe, "Gallows Pole" from Led Zeppelin?"

"All good," Letitia yelled back.

Heather added her vote, and we all grimaced. Heather had the worst taste in music. Her thing was sappy ballads from the seventies. If you let her get to the stereo first, you'd be lucky if she didn't play "Havin' My Baby," or something equally painful. Mercifully, if you beat her to it, she was always fine with your choice.

"Hurry the hell up," I yelled. "Heather is right behind you."

We all started laughing, even Andy, who couldn't have got the joke. It was the mood, the tension of knowing what we were planning to do. The sort of uncomfortable humor that is usually reserved for church or funerals.

As the first notes of "Crazy Train" by Ozzy Osbourn filled the house I smiled. Say what you want about Jake, he always got the music right.

Cassandra's return with the promised chocolate cake didn't reduce the level of silliness. Only narrowed our conversational topics. Not a problem since we had done all the talking we had to for the moment. That didn't keep me from nervously considering the elements of this idea. My first concern was that if Booker paid off his son's debt soon after we ripped off Hugh Rose—assuming we were successful—wouldn't that look damned suspicious? If I was Rose, I'd sure wonder where Booker got the money. I didn't know the man, but it struck me that if he could successfully run a nightclub that was involved in criminal activity, and not get caught, he probably wasn't dumb.

I'd have to think about it some more before talking to Jake. I learned a long time ago that if you're going to mention a problem it's good to offer at least a partial solution. Otherwise, you are basically saying you're a dumb ass and assigning control to someone else.

The other thing bugging me was Jake's state of mind. Back at the house his shaking hands and confession of doing acid worried me. I kept an eye on him all night trying to discern signs that he was sliding into a depression. But I didn't see any. He spent his time laughing with Heather, making jokes with Cassandra, and trading shots of Jägermeister with Little Mikey. He seemed upbeat but that didn't mean much. Jake had always been good at hiding his feelings until it was too late. How often had he seemed to be fine, right up until I found him with a razor in his hand? Too often.

It was easy to think a guy who seemed to have it all must be happy, but I knew better. I wasn't naïve enough to think not having money was better than being rich. But I also knew being rich was different for everyone. The way Jake gave his money away was proof enough that he didn't care that much about it. He'd rather help one of his friends with it than stuff it in a bank. No, money wasn't what drove him. The only thing I think he ever really wanted was to be seen.

I think a lot of us foster kids feel like that. Like we lose our identity when we lose our families. It's easy to believe we're cared for, not because we're loved, but because we provide someone's paycheck. Even the nicest foster parents, like the Sparrows, couldn't provide the same feeling of connection, of shared ancestry. There was always a sense that you were one phone call from being sent away. I guess, to be fair, it's not just limited to foster kids. Every kid wants to be noticed and wants to mean something to someone. Every adult too.

For me, I had to be someone to Zoey. I used to daydream about us being married. The house we'd live in. Our kids. How I'd teach them to fish and hunt, ride a bike, stand up to the bad guys.

Jake had to be someone to his readers. When his first book got published. All that painful stuff he tore out of himself and put on paper was worth it. It meant something. People read him. They saw him. Hard not to. His name was everywhere, on the cover of magazines, on the New York Times Bestseller list. You could hear his voice on podcasts and see his face on the talk shows.

That kind of fame is rare. "Fostering Fear" had been compared to the writing of Tom Wolfe, a master of autobiographical fiction, and to Jack Kerouac, and Hunter Thomson. He wasn't as rich or well-known as say, Stephen King or James Patterson, but he wasn't that far behind. His later books in the thriller genre were popular, though not as popular as his first book, and as the dollars rolled in we mocked him for being bothered by that.

In the short time I'd been back in town I'd never seen him working and he hadn't talked to me about his latest project. Both these things made me suspect he was heading down the well and needed something to interrupt his descent. Helping him steal Hugh Rose's sports memorabilia was likely the best thing I could do for him. When that realization hit me, I put aside all thoughts of trying to talk him out of helping me. Maybe they all needed that sense of being there. Cutting any of them out was a bad idea. I decided the best thing I could do was make the plan as failsafe as possible.

Going into the kitchen, I reluctantly poured my tumbler of scotch down the sink, found a mug, and reached for the coffee pot. If we were going to pull this off, I'd need a clear head.

CHAPTER TWELVE

I expected Hugh Rose would live downtown. He was young, single, and had money so I imagined a loft, maybe in the Pearl. A big echoing space someone like Cassandra had decorated. The sports stuff he collected would hang on the walls.

When the Roses moved to Portland the Pearl was at the peak of being gentrified. Before then it had been a gritty warehouse district called the Northwest Industrial Triangle. Poor artists discovered it and moved in, and soon after art galleries opened, and world-class restaurants showed up. This drew even more people with money. Lots of money.

I was wrong, though. Hugh didn't live in the Pearl. When I entered his name in the county tax assessor's search program two properties came up.

One was owned by O.H. Limo Services with he and his brother listed as partner owners. The other, in his name alone, had an address in Arlington Heights. I'd have to check it out.

The narrow winding roads around his neighborhood made driving Jake's bike a good choice. I had done some research and learned that Arlington Heights is a neighborhood in the Southwest Hills built in the middle of Washington Park. It is close to some of the biggest local attractions, like the Zoo, the Rose Gardens, and the Hoyt Arboretum. The Heights are a thousand feet above the city of Portland and offer a view that doesn't come cheap. I rode slowly past upscale homes in different styles, each on a professionally landscaped lot filled with trees, neatly trimmed lawns, hedges, and flowering things.

Hughs's house was three stories of red brick and white columns, a towering presence that looked like an old-time and badly misplaced plantation house. On each side of the house was a one-story, matching red brick structure. The one on the left was obviously a garage with four overhead doors painted white. The one on the right was more of a mystery. It had a row of tall, barred windows, and a normal exterior door on the side facing the house. In front, a wide driveway circled an island of bushes about knee height. Beside the garage stood a trio of maple trees, their branches trimmed far above head height. That was it as far as natural cover. Not good.

Not wanting to double back and risk being wondered about I found another way out of the neighborhood. I was stewing on the problem of no cover and a house built on the highest point in the area. With its commanding view of the neighborhood, anyone on the property would have a better view of me than I would of it. This was not going to be as easy as I'd thought.

That afternoon we gathered in Jake's media room. Basically, a mini theater. It was an impressive room with a projector screen and two rows of theater seating. Jake used a wireless keyboard to pull up a satellite image of Hugh Rose's house and the surrounding neighborhood.

"The building on the left is obviously a garage," I pointed out.

"Then the one on the right is where he keeps his collection," Andy said. "It's like a small museum."

"How do you know that?" I asked.

"Same way I know everything about him. I've been doing research and man, it's been easy. He's such a media whore. Always in the newspaper showing off this or that."

"There's a pool out back," Jake noted, jiggling the cursor over the blue rectangle on the screen.

"No cover there either," I said, half to myself.

"The guy's got money," Jake said. "That's for damn sure."

"You struggling with taking some of it?" I asked.

"Not really, but it does make it easier to know we aren't going to leave him penniless."

"You guys are funny," said Andy. "Money or not, that guy's a thug. Not all thugs live in ghettos you know."

"They sure don't," Jake agreed. "But I kind of wish this one did. It would probably make it easier. I'm betting he's got security cameras all over the place."

"Well sure," Andy agreed. "Cameras. Detectors. Whatever. But most detectors send a signal that a human has to hear and then respond to. That means there will probably be a lag time in that response. If we time it right, we can be in, get detected, and get out before any kind of response arrives."

"Is that the plan?" I asked him. "Smash, grab, and go?"

"I . . . Well, I don't know," he said, his familiar lack of confidence making an appearance. "I didn't know I was supposed to plan this so I . . ."

"Don't sweat it," said Jake. "We aren't asking you to run things. We just want you to share what you know. Isn't that right?" Jake asked me.

"That's right. I'm going to do the actual job. You and Jake are just here to help with the planning."

Jake's eyes widened. "What?"

"You asked me to do a favor for Letitia. That's what I'm trying to do."

"But I thought we were going to do it together."

"We are. Up to a point. But we don't both need to get hung up if something goes wrong. Besides, didn't you tell me you needed my help so you could do the book tour thing?"

"Well yeah, but we can work around that."

"Uh huh. We'll talk about that later." I planned to outline where Jake could help. But to do that I'd have to push back hard now, so later it felt like I was giving in. Did I like this manipulative stuff? Not at all, but it had to be done if I wanted Jake involved only up to a point. I turned to Andy. "Anyway Andy, Jake's right, I'll do the actual job. I just need you to help me figure out the best way to make it work."

Andy nodded, aware something was going on between Jake and me, but unwilling to step into the middle of it. Smart man. "Okay," he said, "Well then, I need to check out the kind of security system he has. I can't figure out what the best way is until I see what he has. Maybe we'll get lucky, and it'll be something simple, something we can override from a distance and then walk right in."

"Is that a thing?"

"Ask my uncle sunning his butt in Belize. It's a thing."

I nodded and the conversation went on, but I had partly checked out and was thinking about the whole smash-and-grab thing. I liked the idea. The sudden and unexpected seemed like a good way to go.

In the Army, I'd been a mechanic, MOS 91B Wheeled Vehicle Repairer to be exact. Only after a year I got sent to Afghanistan and instead of fixing vehicles, I learned how to demilitarize them which means make them unusable to the enemy. This included working with munitions guys who were there to blow stuff up. By the end of my tour, I had a decent working knowledge of explosives. Reinforced doors and barred windows didn't matter. The right charge in the right place would get us in. Just a matter of not overdoing things and blowing all the goodies to pieces.

So, while they discussed plans, I had already formed mine. Use explosives. Blow the door. Get in, grab what we want, and get out. Sounded easy. But a lot would depend on any additional security measure he had. Did he have bodyguards or guard dogs? Did he carry a gun? When was he at home and when was he gone, and for how long?

These were questions that could only be answered by watching the place over a period of time. The problem was, how? There was no natural cover. No stand of trees. No handy empty home close by. And even if one were, in a neighborhood like this, with cameras everywhere, it wasn't a good idea. There really was no place I could hide unless I wanted to scuba to the bottom of the pool. I looked up and studied the image of the house and neighborhood that was still on the screen.

"Wish we had a live view of that?" I said, mostly to myself.

"What?" Jake asked.

I nodded at the screen.

"Oh, you mean in real-time, like a video feed." Said Jake.

"Or like a drone," said Andy.

"Exactly like a drone," said Jake

We looked at each other.

"Who do we know who has a drone?" I asked him.

"My realtor for one." "When I was looking at houses, she sat me down and showed me several properties. Most of the presentations included overhead views taken by drones. She hired someone to take those, but I don't know if we could hire someone for this sort of thing."

"Not someone legit," Andy said. "Sorry, I don't know anyone."

We sat and thought about it for a moment.

"I'll ask around," Jake finally said. "Make some phone calls."

He told us he had to get some work done, which meant shutting himself in his office down the hall. Being less responsible, and less employed, Andy and I decided to get some lunch.

CHAPTER THIRTEEN

Andy hadn't listened when I told him he wasn't supposed to get too involved. He probably stewed about how he'd seemed shaky about running the show. I jumped right in and told him his participation would be limited. I'm such a fixer of problems. I forget how unobservant I can be. I should have realized that Andy wanted to be seen as necessary just as much as Jake did. That meant he'd want to prove his skills as a burglar. When he said we should get a closer look at the security, I should have heard what he was saying. He was going to get a closer look, no matter what Jake or I said. In a way, I set him up, so he had to prove himself.

It was a nurse who made the call for him. He couldn't talk around the tube in his throat, but he'd managed to get her to find his phone and indicated my number. Jake and I had been sitting on the front stoop of my house. He'd been working all morning, decided to take a break, found me elbows deep in Henry's '57 Chevy, which I'd towed into the driveway the day before, and forced me to join him for a beer. Not much force was needed.

I listened to the nurse, hung up, and looked at Jake who, having overheard some of the conversation, was staring with hawk-like intensity at me. I nodded, confirming his suspicions.

"Andy's hurt. Somebody beat him up. It's bad. He's in the hospital."

"Let's go."

We jumped in Jake's car, and he threw gravel peeling out of the driveway. It wasn't about being in a hurry. It was about being angry. We both knew who had hurt Andy and why.

"They must have caught him sneaking around the place," Jake said.

I nodded but didn't have anything to add. I was equally angry but didn't have the luxury of a fast car to abuse. All I could do was stuff my feelings down deep and hold them there, churning in the pit of my stomach, until it was time to let them out.

The nurse at the desk asked if we were related to Andy. We said yes, we were Andy's brothers. She didn't bat an eye. Nowadays with adoptions and different dads being pretty normal it's a dangerous thing to point out that someone doesn't look like someone else.

Andy was even worse than I'd imagined. One eye looked like he had an eye patch on, only it wasn't a patch, it was his eyelid, hugely swollen and dark purple. The rest of his face was mottled red and pink, and another dark bruise covered the left side of his jaw. His right hand was wrapped in a bandage while his left was in a partial cast that covered his wrist, pinkie and ring finger.

"Dr. Hershiser will be here in about an hour if you want to talk to her," the nurse offered.

"Can you tell me anything?" I practically begged. "What's wrong with him? What happened?"

"What happened? I don't think anyone knows for certain. All we were told is that someone saw him staggering along the shoulder on Sunset Highway and called the police. When they realized he wasn't drunk they called an ambulance. They think someone pushed him out of a car, not moving thank God, and that he'd been in a fight. He has injuries that suggest a fistfight and that someone stomped him with boots. There are boot-shaped bruises on his chest, back, and legs. He has three broken ribs, and someone stomped his hand hard enough to break two fingers. Whatever happened to your brother, it wasn't pleasant. He asked me to call you and he was conscious for a while, but the doctors decided it would be best to place him in an induced coma, mostly to help get him past the worst of the pain. You probably won't be able to talk to him for another day or two." She looked at her watch. "I have to go. I can have someone bring in another chair if you'd like." She gestured to the single chair in one corner of the narrow room.

I shook my head. “Thanks, but we aren’t staying that long.”

“Okay, well if you change your mind just ask someone at the desk.” With that she slipped out of the room, leaving Jake and I with our anger, our questions, and our guilt.

“Kid looks bad. He’s all busted up. Can’t let this stand,” said Jake.

Andy had been peripheral to the family but no more. I could see the look on Jake’s face. The look he saved for family. A mix of affection and pride when he stared down at Andy’s broken body. And when he met my eyes a look of undisguised rage that nearly reached the level of mine.

Without a word we turned and left Andy’s room. Left behind the hiss of his machine assisted breathing and the welcome sound of his heartbeat pulsing through another machine.

Outside again we walked toward the car, and I let the hot anger bubble up. I’m going to find who did that to him and tear them apart. Then I’m going to find Rose and . . .”

"You're not going to do any of that. At least not yet. If you do our chance to get Letitia and Booker free of this mess is gone. Last time you went off without thinking it cost you a year. You ready to give up more time?"

I was not.

I got in the car and took a deep breath. Everyone always tells you to take a deep breath, count to ten. Not sure any of that ever helped. I turned on the radio and twisted the volume up. Machine Head's "Ten Ton Hammers" slammed me back in my seat. Jake slapped the radio off.

"No. That will just make you worse. Settle down or I'll put on some of that nice music Heather likes."

"I just want to hurt them, not kill them," I said.

Jake smiled. "You could be right." He put the music back on at a less ear bleed level and as we pulled out of the hospital's parking garage my mind filled with pleasing scenes of mayhem.

"You know, we don't know for sure what happened to Andy. What if it wasn't Rose?"

I made a snorting sound. "Really?"

"I know. Odds are pretty good it was them, but we should know for sure before we do anything. Can you stay cool until Andy can talk to us?"

As I nodded my agreement the lyrics, "like broken glass you'll shatter, with bloody fists I'll batter, like a ten-ton hammer son", declared my intentions much better than I could.

I think, more to distract me than anything, Jake decided to call for a war council of sorts. He wanted to bring those of us together who were involved. That meant that the next afternoon Letitia, Tilly, and the two of us met at my place. It was easier to protect Cassandra from our plans if we weren't at the house. And though they were a big part of this, we didn't invite Booker and his son. We weren't sure just how much we could trust them, especially Booker if it meant protecting his son, and besides, they weren't family.

We told Letitia and Tilly what had happened to Andy. Then had to spend several minutes convincing

Letitia that it wasn't her fault. That in fact we weren't even sure of the facts.

"I wish the drones had been in place, so we'd have real proof it was Hugh Rose and his guys who did that to him," said Jake.

"I don't really need a video to tell me what happened," I said. "I know he wanted a look at the security system. I know he snuck up on the house and someone saw him. They caught him, dragged him into the house or back yard, anyway out of view of the neighbors and they put the boots to him. Then they loaded him into a car and dumped him on the highway. They could have killed him."

"That's probably what happened," Jake agreed, but we can't do anything until we're sure. Andy will be awake soon. You heard the nurse. We'll ask him and then we'll act. I'm not doing anything until I'm sure and you shouldn't either. That's not who we are."

I sat there, on the couch Heather or Cassandra had chosen, in the house Jake owned and wondered just who this *we* he imagined was. Someone fresh out of jail, mooching on his friends, who way too often woke up alone in a cold sweat scared of something that wasn't even there. Jake was a successful man with a cult following of fans, a beautiful, educated girlfriend, and friends he'd helped along the way. There was no we. There was Jake and there was me. And me was pissed.

"Well, working on the assumption that Hugh Rose is responsible, what are we going to do about it?" asked Jake.

"That's easy," said Letitia.

"How's that?"

"Money, babe. It's all about the money. It's the only way you can hurt someone like that. He has no woman, no kids. He might give a damn about his brother, but I tend to doubt it. Everybody has a point of pride. Me. I gotta prove I'm smart. Someone in the room smarter than me, which happens more than I like, and it gets under my skin like an itch. I don't like it. In school I had to have the best grades. Other things, not so much. I used to run track. I tried to be the best, but I didn't try try you know? But getting those grades. That was important. My point of pride. So, what is this guys?"

"Well, Andy said he could learn all he wanted about him because of his bragging in the papers and magazines about his sports collection. The biggest and best in the area he claims. He built a damn museum to house the stuff. He has a bodyguard that stays on the property to keep an eye on it. He got his guys to almost kill Andy 'cause he sniffed around it." Here I shot a look at Jake to acknowledge that wasn't a certainty yet.

"I see," said Letitia. So, if you want to hurt me show me someone with a better IQ. You want to hurt him? Take his collection away."

I thought we agreed to take only what would replace what he stole, a hundred thousand or so?" said Jake.

"That was before Andy," said Letitia. "I get what you're saying Jake. God knows I have no right to say anything about any of this since I'm the one got us here, got Andy here for that matter."

"Don't start that again," said Jake.

Letitia brushed him off. "I'm with Bobby on this. This is a double-dealing nasty bastard who doesn't deserve our restraint. Not after what he did to the Robinsons and me and sure as hell not after what he did to Boby's friend, Andy. We need to hurt him back."

"If he did it," said Jake

"Right. If he did it. If Andy comes to and tells us they were responsible, then the gloves come off."

I liked that. Letitia taking the gloves off. She was a force to be reckoned with and I was happy she was on our side.

"It won't hurt to have a plan," Letitia said, "Just in case we're not wrong."

After that we got down to details. We knew a few things. According to Howie, Hugh Rose worked mostly from home but on Saturday nights, around midnight and until closing, he liked to make an appearance at his nightclub. He usually took one of his guys with him.

Also, according to Howie, that meant only two men at the house on Saturday night, one thug and one maintenance guy. I didn't discount the maintenance guy's capacity for thuggery, knowing who he worked for.

We ended up with a simple plan. The best ones usually are. We'd wait until one in the morning. That time when Hugh would be gone and the people at the house were probably asleep. Jake would drive up and park in the street. The car would be out of sight unless someone looked out of an upper story window. I'd run up, plant an explosive on the side door to the building, duck around to the front and blow the door. Then I'd run inside and grab everything I could find and shove it into a duffel bag. I'd carry a ball peen hammer in case there was glass to break.

Some crazy thing inside had me hoping there was lots of glass. The more rational part of me said all his treasures were probably behind sun blocking plexiglass. That would come under the same category as opening one of those plastic-wrapped products, like a shaving razor. The kind of wrapping that defies you to remove it. Couldn't be helped but I did have to think about it some more. Maybe talk to Andy again.

That's how we left it. We'd take all the things that meant the most to Hugh Rose. Letitia would get her money back. Booker would buy his son's career and freedom. The money would help Andy out too. Maybe help him get a fresh start doing something other than burglary. It sounded a little risky and a lot exciting. It felt good. Like things were going to work out.

"I'll call the hospital and check on him in the morning," I said, as everyone got up to leave. "If there's a change, I'll let you all know."

Tilly gave me a quick hug and then Letitia. Only Letitia's hug had her wrapping one slender leg around mine and her arms around my neck.

"Stop trying to climb the man," Tilly said, giving Letitia a resounding smack on the ass.

"Hey, that hurt!" Letitia said, abruptly letting me go and turning to her partner. "I think I liked it."

"Well let's go home and find out how much."

"Sluts. We've got a room full of sluts," said Jake.

"Lucky bastards," said Letitia and her and Jake laughed like crazy people. Tilly and I looked at each other and shook our heads.

That was how we left it. A plan to smash, grab, and run like hell. It wasn't Andy's way, but I liked it.

Everything seemed to be coming together.

And then Jake disappeared.

CHAPTER FOURTEEN

In the morning I called the hospital and was told they planned to bring Andy out of his chemically induced coma that afternoon. I called Jake but the call went to voice mail, so I left a message, then called Letitia to let her know.

"Will you call me before you go to the hospital.," she said. "I'd like to meet you there, bring some flowers or something. I know you guys tried to convince me it wasn't my fault, but even if it wasn't, he's a nice guy and I owe him at least that much. Do you think he'd like a card?"

"I guess."

"How about a card with some naked shots of my ass?"

"We want to cure him, not kill him."

"You are no fun," she said, and I could imagine her phony pout.

"I'll call you when I leave. I'll probably pick up Jake too."

"Okay, T T Y L she said into the phone, as if she were leaving a text, and hung up.

I tried Jake again and got the same result. No answer.

I worked on Henry's Chevy for a while, but I couldn't concentrate. Inside, I washed up and switched on the television then clicked through the choices. Angy local politics. Depressing world news. Sitcoms with canned laugh tracks or prompted audiences that made my nerves jangle. I'd have to figure out where the closest library was and stock up on some reading material.

I was jolted out of my drowsiness by the beeping sound of a truck reversing somewhere nearby. As I struggled to gather my bearings, I realized that I was no longer on the couch but instead caught in a familiar nightmare. My surroundings were pitch black. I was trapped within the narrow confines of what was little more than a hollow in the rocky cliff face, barely big enough to accommodate my huddled form.

My shoulders were squeezed tightly together, and my knees were drawn up to my chest, leaving me feeling trapped and claustrophobic. My hips ached from sitting in the same uncomfortable position for what felt like an eternity, but I dared not move. The darkness around me was suffocating, and the silence was deafening. It was as if time had stood still, and I was suspended in a void with no way out.

I'd been taking the communication equipment out of the cab of an overturned Humvee. Kirk, the explosives guy, had been checking for the best place to plant some C4 and blow the sucker up. It was just for laughs. That gun truck wasn't going to move again. It had rolled over an IED and from the dried blood stains in the cab the driver wasn't functioning anymore either. I'd probably made a joke about it back then. Not because I didn't give a shit, but because I did.

A shot rang out and I both heard and felt Kirk's body slam against the truck as the impact slapped him forward. I dropped onto the ground behind the truck and waited for the burst of firing that was sure to follow. When nothing happened, I worked my way backward until I was able to roll into a rocky ditch. That ditch was my only hope. If I could stay low and crawl, I might get away from the truck and anyone firing at it. But first, I had to make sure Kirk wasn't still alive and in need of my help. So, against all instinct, once I dropped into the ditch, I crawled, not away, but toward the front of the truck.

The upper part of Kirk's body had tumbled into the ditch and as I crept closer, I saw that his eyes were open and looking up unseeing at the empty blue sky. The sky wasn't that empty though. In the distance, a thin line of brown dust was rising into the air. Around me, nothing stirred. Behind me, our vehicle's engine ticked. The metallic ping of a cooling engine filled my senses. Kirk had been driving and he had the keys. Could I get them and get into our truck and away?

The telltale curl of dust from a vehicle racing toward me made up my mind. Even if I could get to the truck in time, I was pretty sure I couldn't outrun or avoid a barrage of bullets. The fucking Haji were known for their utter lack of frugality when it came to throwing bullets around

Not far from the Humvee was a cluster of rocks fallen from a low cliff that marked the start of sandy-covered foothills that climbed toward a peak in the distance. Maybe I could hunker behind the rocks and work my way around the cliff. The wind brought the sound of men's yelling voices. I ran up and out of the ditch keeping low, scuttling like a damn crab across the ground. As soon as I got past the rocks, I saw the shadows at the base of the cliff. Holes that seemed ripped from the rock wall. My fevered imagination saw them as gaping holes in torn flesh.

Without a second thought, I darted towards one of the shadowy spaces and pushed myself inside. The opening was narrow, and I had to struggle to get my body through. Once in I turned so that my back was to the wall, then I reached up and started clawing at the overhanging rocks and soil. A few moments later, there was a sharp crack, and the earth above me crumbled and fell. It hit my head and arms, burying me alive under a heap of sand.

Desperately, I cupped my hand over my nose, forming a tiny pocket of air to breathe as more dirt and small rocks slid from above. I waited until I thought I was completely covered, then used the first two fingers of my other hand to claw at the dirt, creating a small hole just big enough for me to gasp for air through the gaps between my fingers. The sand was gritty against my skin, and my heart pounded in my chest, but I knew I had to stay calm if I wanted to remain hidden and make it out alive.

Despite the muffled quality of the sound, I could still hear a commotion outside. The sound of a truck rolling up was followed by a chorus of doors slamming shut and men shouting, their voices growing louder by the minute. By their victorious voices I knew without a doubt that they had found Kirk's body.

Sweat trickled down my side, and I shivered uncontrollably, causing a thin cascade of sand to slip to the ground. My heart pounded with fear as I wondered whether they had heard me or if I was fully hidden from view. The uncertainty was unbearable, but all I could do was stay still, take shallow breaths, and wait.

I waited there for what felt like an eternity, enduring the long day and the even longer night. The sun rose and set, and still, I dared not move, listening for any sign that they might be closing in on me. My muscles ached from being still for so long, but I knew that any sudden movement could mean the end of my life. I had to remain patient and stay hidden until the right moment presented itself.

When the sun went down the temperature fell with it. It was so cold I couldn't help but shiver and this sent more sand and rocks tumbling to the desert floor. My legs cramped; spasms so painful they almost drove me to my feet. I clenched my teeth and waited them out.

With my head tilted forward I was able to clear the sand from my eyes. Through the narrow slits I saw the flickering light of their fire. It was so near, with a promise of warmth that called to me. I shut my eyes and thought about Zoey. How we'd hitched to Diamond Lake and spent a whole day jumping into the freezing water, shivering and laughing. How we'd made love in a grassy meadow our bodies hot and slick with sweat. Is it crazy to believe memories of her warm, soft body kept me alive?

In the morning it was quiet. The voices stilled while everyone slept. I considered leaving my hidey hole. Trying that original plan to work my way around the cliff but I couldn't recall how far away that was and I was fairly certain they'd have someone standing guard. I would have. So, I waited.

The sun rose, lifting a little of the darkness and with it my spirits. It was a primitive feeling, but then I was a primitive thing performing the most basic function. Hiding from my enemy. Surviving.

Gradually, the temperature rose. Here in the desert, it could get over one hundred degrees Fahrenheit during the day. I could literally feel the touch of the sun as it reached my shelter. First, it warmed my feet, then my knees, and then my entire body stopped shaking from the cold becoming comfortable, then warm, and then hot, hot as all the levels of hell. Sand made every square inch of my damp skin itch. Sweat stung my eyes and ran down my body in rivulets. Most of all I was thirsty. The idea of water became all I could think of. I told myself to think of something else. Anything else. But even thoughts of Zoey could not ease the growing demand for water.

As the hours dragged on, the men outside began to stir from their sleep, their voices growing clearer and more discernible. But even then, I could only make out every fifth word, making it impossible for me to decipher what they were saying.

At one point, the sound of a rock rolling under someone's foot made me flinch. A moment later, I heard the tell-tale sound of someone urinating, and my heart skipped a beat. My mind conjured up images of a man with a rifle slung over his shoulder, lifting the weapon and firing a shot into my hiding place. The thought of dying was terrifying, but even more so was the idea that my time spent in this hell would be for nothing.

I needed to stay calm, to take deep breaths and control the rising panic in my chest. I had to focus on the mission, on surviving this ordeal, and finding a way out. I knew that if I let fear take over, it would be the end of me. I forced myself to think only of the spots of light under my closed eyelids. I imagined I was diving into a narrow channel between the bars of light, and when I broke from that thought I forced myself to do it again. My breathing slowed. I became still. In a few moments, I heard the man's retreating footsteps. I was safe. For the moment.

More hours passed and just as I decided I had to move or go insane I heard the slam of doors and the grind of a starter. They were leaving. I was going to wait a little longer and give them time to get far away, but my body disagreed. I stood up and instantly fell. It was okay. The truck was moving away fast, and it was loud, covered with hillbilly armor made from scavenged parts it rattled and jangled covering any sound I might have made. I rolled onto my back and stared at the miraculous sky. No bed had ever felt as good as that stretch of sand. No air ever tasted as sweet.

The phone rang and rang again, sending out an acoustic guitar riff I found less annoying than most ringtones. The sound pulled me from the past and into the now. I woke up with gratitude, blinking and yawning as the nightmare faded with the light.

CHAPTER FIFTEEN

I had expected Jake would be the caller, but it was Cassandra. Her unexpected voice shook off the last of the haze.

"Hi Bobby, is Jake with you by any chance?"

"Uh, no. I haven't seen him today."

"Okay. Well, I'm in Eugene. I got called in yesterday to cover a trial for a sick colleague. Usually, when I'm away like this, Jake and I talk at lunchtime. He probably just forgot to charge his phone or something. I'll call him later. Thanks."

"No problem," I said and heard the click as she hung up.

It wasn't a big deal. The anxiety in her voice was just my imagination. What she said was probably right. Jake had forgotten to charge his phone. Sure, when his girlfriend was away, and he was in the middle of planning a burglary. That's the time he'd forget. It didn't sound like him. Jake was way more wedded to the tech stuff, phones and computers, and whatnot than I was. I wasn't exactly worried, but little pings of something were going off.

They'd said Andy would be brought out of his coma this afternoon. I looked at the clock on my phone. Just past noon. Probably too early. I'd give it an hour and then call the hospital. I was so bored I'd drifted off so might as well get on the bike and run over to Jakes. Be a friend and let him know his girlfriend was looking for him.

Pulling into Jakes's driveway about half an hour later I knew he wasn't there. I don't know what it is that tells you a house is empty. Maybe the lack of sound we pick up on some subconscious level. In any case, I went ahead and knocked and rang the bell, just in case those finely honed instincts of mine were wrong. They weren't.

I sat in one of the two rocking chairs on the wide front porch and thought about things I didn't want to think about. I'd thought being involved in helping me recover Letitia's stuff, even if that involvement was limited, would keep Jake focused on something outside himself, but I'd seen the signs. Maybe he was somewhere buying coffee beans, or beer, or hitting the library. His favorite hang as a kid.

A sense of foreboding was growing and making me restless. Maybe it was only an after-effect of my flashback to the cave. Reliving the scene that I knew was probably the main contributor to the post-traumatic bullshit I'd been diagnosed with had to mess with me, at least for a while. Or maybe Jake was dropping acid or downing handfuls of pills and chugging top-shelf whiskey. It wouldn't be the first time. If he was, then I knew where I could find him.

I got on the bike and threw out a rooster tail of gravel as I ripped out of the driveway. More certain with every moment that when I found Jake, he'd be dead. I raced to the duplex and into Jake's office and used his computer to search for property he owned. I was never more grateful for the tax man, who keeps a public list of property owners, than when I quickly found a property in the rural town of Mist in Jake's name.

He'd told me about his getaway place. A remote bit of land with an old falling-down house and barn. If he was contemplating doing something stupid, I was betting that's where he'd do it.

I took 26 West to 47 North. The landscape changing from city to suburb to country. If I'd been in a different state of mind I'd have enjoyed the ride and the scenery.

An hour later my phone's GPS told me I'd found the entrance to Jake's property. The driveway was narrow and crossed a creek, curved past some trees, blocking the view of the house from the main road. It had once been a nice two-story farmhouse. Now it leaned slightly, its windows gone. No one had bothered to tack plywood over the open frames. Vines had crept up the sides making it look like some post-apocalyptic image of nature regaining ground.

Beyond the house was the barn. I could see blue sky through gaps in the vertical wood siding, but the roof looked new. The gleam of sun reflecting from the polished paint on Jake's Chevy parked in front of it caught my eye. I pulled up next it, got off, and practically ran to the wide doors, which stood open.

Coming inside from the bright day into the shadowy barn I didn't see him at first. Then my eyes adjusted, and I gave a huge sigh of relief. Jake was standing in front of a long wooden workbench, bent over a block of wood held in a vice. He was using a hammer and chisel and didn't stop as I approached. Even though the wide plank floors should have telegraphed my footsteps. I quickly realized he couldn't hear me. A set of earbuds told me he was listening to music and knowing him it was probably cranked to ear bleed level.

I stood behind him, arms crossed until the weight of my glare broke through and he turned around, startled a moment, and then smiled.

"Dude," he said, sounding like Andy. He took out the earbuds and I caught the sound of a vaguely familiar tune and then nothing as he shoved them into his pocket. "What are you doing here?"

It took a determined moment not to say something honest like, I was worried about you or, you scared the shit out of me, or I broke every land speed record getting here and for nothing. Instead, I shrugged and said, “Wanted to go for a ride and Cassandra called looking for you so thought I’d ride out here.”

“Yeah, my phone died. Not just the battery. The whole damn thing just shut down for no good reason. I ordered a new one this morning. Should be here this afternoon. The wonders of online shopping never cease to amaze. You been worrying about Andy?”

I nodded. If that’s what he wanted to believe, I’d let him.

“What are you doing?” I asked, nodding toward the bench.

“Learning to carve. I’ve been taking an online course. This is the second project, a fish, salmon to be specific.”

I stepped closer and could vaguely see the form of a fish being carved from the block of wood. “Why a fish?” I asked.

“Easiest form. Or anyway, that’s what the teacher said. Cass and I were at a gallery not long ago and there was this carving with seaweed and a couple of fish sort of leaping. She liked it so I thought I’d try to make her one, like maybe for a birthday present or something."

"Nice."

"Sure, if she still likes the same stuff when she's sixty. That's about how long it's going to take to make this. I just accidentally cut a fin off. It's going to be a lot skinnier fish than I planned on."

"Maybe it was a lean year," I offered, unable to keep the smile that wasn't exactly sympathy off my face."

"You're not helping."

"I rarely do."

Not long after, we headed back to town. Jake drove ahead and I followed a few car lengths behind. I was in no hurry. Back in the day an open road with little traffic would have meant a race between us. We'd have taken stupid chances in the name of competitiveness. Maybe we were older and wiser. Or maybe there were just more things to think about.

It was early afternoon when we reached Jake's house. I called the hospital and was told that yes, Andy was conscious and yes, he could have visitors.

Andy looked bad but better. His face was still black and blue, but the swelling had gone down some. At least he could open both eyes and he smiled when he saw us.

"Andy," I said, "What the hell did they do to you?"

"Ah dude," he said, his voice full of gravel and strained. "I just went to check out how to get into the place. Big guy with muscles jumped me. Hit me in the back of the head. I think with his fist. Knocked me loopy. Next thing I know I'm out by the pool and him and another guy are kicking the crap out of me. Muscles kicked me in the head, and I blacked out. Next thing I know I'm looking at some cop's shoes in tall grass. It's been strange."

"They dumped you on the side of the road," I told him. "Someone called the cops, probably thinking you were on drugs or drunk and worried you'd wander into traffic. The cops called an ambulance. Did they tell you you've been here for two days?"

He nodded. Jake had walked around to the other side of the bed and poured water into a glass from a mustard yellow pitcher that was there. He handed it to Andy who nodded his appreciation and took a long drink, sipping from a plastic straw. His movements were slow, and he winced as he reached to hand the glass back to Jake.

"Hand's going to heal fine. The worst is my back. Couldn't feel my legs at first but now I got some tingling. Doc says probably swelling in my spine. Not permanent. Got lucky. Should have listened to you, dude. Should have stayed away. Don't know how I'm gonna pay for this. Didn't learn much anyway."

"That's okay," I told him. "We're going with plan A. Screw taking what he took. I'm gonna bust down the door and grab every damn thing I can before I go."

"I can help. I've been studying pictures of the place in the papers," he said. "I know the layout. Inside on the right is a wet bar. On the far end, to the left, is a pool table, with some chairs against the wall around it. Most the stuff we want is on the walls on shelves or in frames. Take a bag, go right to left or left to right and work your way around and out of the room. Just take what's easiest." He coughed. His voice was getting hoarser by the moment. "I did find out something else that might help. Arrogant prick has security on the door but nothing on the windows. He figures bars are enough. He's a dumb ass. You should go through the window. Take what you can and don't worry about value. It's all valuable. Go fast. When you get back to the window climb out and run like hell. I know you got this Bobby. I know you're gonna make that fucker pay."

"I will," I promised. "Not a doubt."

"Good. Now I just gotta worry how I'm gonna pay for this," he said.

"Don't worry about it," said Jake. "I'll talk to the hospital. See what kind of financial aid they have. Most hospitals that take federal funds have—"

He said more but I wasn't listening. Since realizing that Andy was going to be all right, I had begun an inner dialogue. Until now I'd felt nothing but the gathering anger twisting in the pit of my stomach. Now I fought it down. Blind rage is exactly that, blind. This was not the time. I had to be calm enough, cool enough, to inflict the largest amount of pain and loss that I could.

CHAPTER SIXTEEN

On the drive home from the hospital, Jake and I decided to call another planning meeting. This time, thinking the more brains the better, we invited everyone, and everyone came. Because Cassandra was still out of town we met at Jake's where his giant kitchen table could accommodate everyone. We were a somber group. Jake was serious and unsmiling. Booker and his son, Nathan, looked nervous. Letitia and Tilly were quiet. The only one that didn't seem depressed or anxious was Heather. She pulled yarn and a hook out of a giant bag at her feet and began crocheting flowers, yellow with black centers. As she finished each one, she snipped off the yarn with a pair of tiny scissors that looked like a skinny bird.

Watching her work had a calming effect on me.

Jake and I told them about Andy's condition, that Rose and his men were responsible, and that he'd suggested a plan for the burglary. After I laid it out Booker said, "Not much of a plan. What if they respond faster than you think? What will you do if they come barreling out of the house and start shooting? You say that place is a damn fortress. They catch you in there it would be like shooting fish in a barrel."

"A big brick barrel," said Jake.

The others nodded their agreement.

"I'm still working it out," I told them. They could say what they wanted, and offer their help, but at the end of the day, this was my job and my plan. "I won't do anything until I've got a pretty good chance at success."

"Success means you won't get caught, right?" asked Heather.

"That's right," I said.

"Well, I was thinking about that," she said, and put the flower she was working on down on the table. Then she reached into the bag at her feet and pulled out a couple large Ziplock freezer bags. "I brought these." She opened the bags and pulled wigs out of one and masks from the other. “I bet they have cameras, so I thought you better wear a disguise.”

I couldn’t resist and took the darkest wig and tugged it onto my head. It was long, curly and had been tied into a ponytail. Jake snickered. “You know who you look like? He’s gonna think he got ripped off by Howard Stern.”

“Seriously?” I asked. I had to see. There was a mirror near the front door. I took one look and laughed as hard as anyone. “Just need some sunglasses and I’m ready for Halloween,” I told them, as I returned to the kitchen.

The laughter changed the vibe of the room. It was us again. A strange group of people thrown together by fate who had become friends, if not family.

I tried on the second wig. This one was closer to my own brown hair but much longer. It had also been tied into a ponytail.

“I didn’t think you’d want hair in your face,” explained Heather. And look. I brought masks too.”

There were three of them. One was featureless and white with slits for the eyes, nose, and mouth. Another was a Guy Fawkes mask, with recognizable arched eyebrows, mustache, and soul patch from the V for Vendetta movie. The third was a Jason-style hockey mask.

"You can pick whatever one you're in the mood for. See, Jason if you're mad. Guy if you're looking for revenge, or the plain one if you just want to hide who you are. You have lots of options."

"They're awesome," I told her, and meant it. What a thoughtful thing to do. I didn't tell her I wouldn't be wearing one of them. I'd been a kid who loved to dress up for Halloween. I knew how hard those masks were to breathe or see through. Not the thing for this kind of job. The medical masks I'd taken from Andy's hospital room would do the job. The brown wig? Yeah, I'd wear that. Why not?

Letitia put on the Guy Fawkes mask and started vamping, twirling an invisible mustache for effect. The doorbell rang and we all froze, looking like the guiltiest people in the world. Not a poker face among us. Jake was the first to move.

"Probably UPS or something," he muttered as he headed toward the front door.

When he came back Little Mikey was with him.

"Heard you guys were having a powwow so thought I'd join in."

Little Mikey could get away with saying powwow because he was Native American, a combination of Apache, and Comanche. "Two tribes that hated each other, which explains so much about my parent's marriage," he'd told me once. Mikey stayed at the Sparrow's off and on. Off when at least one of his parents was sober. On when both had fallen off the wagon.

"Who told you we were meeting?" I asked, annoyed by the level of anxiety prickling through my nerves.

"Andy. Went to see him a little while ago. Kid looks like shit. Thought maybe you'd like some help making those assholes look worse."

"Help's always welcome," I said.

"Hey Mikey," said Heather.

"Hey. What's that you're doing?"

"Making flowers to sew onto some retro sweaters I picked up. The sixties and seventies are hot right now."

"That's cool," said Little Mikey, sounding sincerely interested, or at least like he was trying to.

He'd always had a thing for Heather, but his chances were not good. To Heather, the world was divided into only two types of people, friends, and others. I don't think she had a category for boyfriends, girlfriends, or lovers of any sort.

We brought Little Mikey up to speed and then Booker entered the conversation for the first time. "I think we have another problem."

"Yeah, what's that?" asked Jake.

"Me and Nathan were talking about it and it occurred to us that—well say we pull this off. We rip off a bunch of stuff from Mr. Rose. Then you sell it and give me enough to clear Nathan's debt with Mr. Miller. He works for Rose, and I'll bet he'll know about the burglary. Then, suddenly there I am paying him off. You think he won't put two and two together?"

We all thought about it and realized that yes, he'd put it together and that would make all the masks and wigs and sneaking worth nothing.

"Hey, don't look so down," he told us. "Me and Nathan, we came up with a solution."

"He shouldn't do it," said Nathan. "I told him he shouldn't. I'm the one screwed up. I'm the one should pay."

"What are you talking about?" asked Letetia.

"He wants to sell the house," said Nathan. "His damn house. He loves that place."

"Well, love. That's a strong word," said Booker.

"No, it ain't. That house is more than just a house and you know it. You told me so how many times?"

Seeing our expressions, Booker explained. "Back in the early 1900's the neighborhood where my house is, Laurelhurst, had this rule about developing the area. It said nobody could occupy a house there if they were Chinese, Japanese, or negroes, except for one exception. Those kinds of folks could be live in servants of the residents."

"No shit?" said Letitia.

"No shit," said Nathan.

"It's one of the reasons I bought a house there. Hell, even as late as the 30's there was a map that showed the tracts as desirable partly because the area had no foreign-born or black inhabitants. It gives me no end of pleasure to be a black inhabitant. Even though truth be told, I'm more a sort of light roast," he said with a smile.

No one laughed.

"Anyway," he continued, "I'll say the money came from the sale of the house. Actually, it *will* come from that. It's too much house anyway, now Nathan's mom has moved out and he'll be going on his way soon too. There's a new apartment complex over on the river. If I move fast, I can put a deposit on a unit that faces the water. One of my friends lives nearby and my favorite restaurant is two blocks away. This is all stuff I told Nathan but he's not seeing it. He doesn't get that when you get old you want less stuff and more time."

I wasn't sure I was buying it either. Booker was talking like he was ancient, but he wasn't all that old. I'd peg him as somewhere in his late forties, early fifties. It didn't matter if he was lying to make it easier for his son to accept the idea. His idea was a good one and would keep Hugh Rose from having another excuse to come at him.

"I think that's smart. It'll still piss Rose off because what he really wants is for you to throw a game," Jake said to Nathan. "Because then he'll own you. But your dad is going to take away that option. That, along with taking his toys, is going to make me, for one, feel real good."

I didn't think Nathan particularly cared if Jake felt good or not, but he didn't say a word. Smart kid. As he'd acknowledged, he was the one that dragged his father into this mess, dragged all of us, really. He'd be smart to sit there and be quiet while the grownups figured it out. Felt weird to be one of the grownups though. "Let's get started," I said.

I was the note taker this time, bent over one of Jake's yellow legal pads, scribbling ideas as fast as they were tossed to me. It was Little Mikey who gave me the best one.

CHAPTER SEVENTEEN

Saturday night the moon was waning, a thin crescent dimmed by the city lights. The sky was dark, but the neighborhood wasn't. Porch and streetlamps lit things up nicely with only pockets of shadow here and there. But it was also still. The dogs all lived indoors with their owners. Pampered pooches snoozing away. Not a single warning bark or growl to be heard as Jake and I drove into the neighborhood and parked half a block away.

Unlike Hugh Rose's austere grounds, his neighbor's place had an eight-foot-tall, four-foot-wide hedge, symmetrical blocks of green on both sides of a pair of wrought iron gates. Jake parked in front of the nearest hedge, and we sat a moment looking around for a glimpse of a curtain being pulled back or a light going on. There was nothing.

I wanted to go in quiet, so we'd made some precautions. Jake had left his distinctive Chevy Malibu at home, and we were in his old college car, a dark blue Toyota Corolla. I'd watched him swap out the plates. I didn't ask him why he had an extra set.

"Doesn't hurt to be cautious," he said. He also unscrewed the bulb from the ceiling light. When we opened a door we wouldn't be lit up. Nonetheless, we were in disguise. Jake had opted to wear the Howard Stern hair and I was in the brown ponytail. Now, I slipped on the dark blue medical mask and a pair of black leather driving gloves. The black canvas duffel bag was at my feet with the tools I thought I might need in a side pocket.

We sat for a moment longer, windows rolled down, listening to the sounds of an ordinary, if slightly more expensive, suburban neighborhood. Then it was go time. I got out, eased the door shut, and moved across the island of grass to the sidewalk. Mica in the concrete sparkled under the ambient light. I could smell a sweet floral scent and realized it was coming from clusters of small white flowers on the hedge.

I reached the brick building that held Rose's treasures. The doors had security alarms but the windows, as far as Andy could tell, only had bars. "That's lucky," Little Mikey had explained. "If it was a new place that would be bad, but it's old, so yeah, lucky."

"How so?" Jake had asked.

"In new construction, the bars are embedded in concrete. You basically have to bust out the concrete to remove them. In old construction, the bars are usually screwed into the wooden frame of the window. They probably used special tamper-proof screws that can't be unscrewed without a special tool."

"Which you have?" I asked.

"No."

"Then, pardon the pun, but we're screwed," said Jake.

"Not really. Because you're not going to unscrew them."

Now, standing in front of the window at three in the morning, a pen light between my teeth, I carefully applied a small amount of valve grinding compound to the first screw, picked up the drill, muffled with foam and liable to overheat and die quickly, and pressed the bit against the head of the screw. Instead of trying to back the tamper-proof screw out, which wouldn't have worked, I tightened it more and more until I felt a sudden lack of friction. It worked. The screw had worn out the wood fibers around it and lost its tension. Now it just spun inside the hole. I would have to repeat that seven more times. To reach the high ones I'd brought a step ladder. I worked fast and though it was chilly, with a damp wind that promised rain, I was sweating by the time I'd removed the third screw.

"Figure half to a full minute for each screw and a couple more for problems," Mikey had said. "Shouldn't take more than ten minutes. Wouldn't hurt to take an extra drill in case the first one overheats and quits working." He said this while grabbing another drill out of a tool bag he'd brought to my apartment. "If you need to leave them behind don't worry about it. No prints and untraceable. You'll need some kind of ladder or step stool. Make sure you wipe it down with some white vinegar before you put it in the car and after that only touch it with your gloves on."

"I thought Andy was the expert criminal," I joked.

"Before I got into electrical work for construction, I used to install security systems," Mikey explained. "That's how I worked my way through school. My boss always said you had to know what the criminals know if you want to stop them."

"Yeah, I kind of remember that now. And here I was thinking I was surrounded by crooks."

Little Mikey laughed, "Oh, you are. Don't you worry about that. I've met your friends."

Stripping out the eight screws took a little less than ten minutes. The next step was to switch the drill bit for an extractor bit. The bit had little sharp burrs that dug into the metal of the screw. I used it on the five stubborn ones that refused to be pulled out with my fingers. Once I twisted them out far enough, I slipped the tip of a flat screwdriver behind the head and pried them out.

When I was done the bars were held in place only by old layers of paint. I wrapped my hands around them and tugged several times. When they resisted, I used my pocketknife to dig into the paint. On the fourth attempt, with a sort of sucking noise, the bars finally came free, and I lowered them onto the grass.

With no time to waste, I began working on the window. The old-fashioned sash windows had two movable panes of glass. I didn't want to break them. Breaking glass always gets attention. It's a sound that all people seem to find disturbing. I'd already noticed the window beading that Mikey had talked to me about. I took up the paint scraper again and used it to pry off the beading around the lower windowpane. In no time I was removing the entire pane of glass. I set it down and leaned it carefully against the side of the structure. No alarms. Unless there was a silent one going off somewhere. I used the stepladder to easily climb through the window, feeling for the ground and finally dropping a short couple of feet to the floor.

As Andy had predicted, when I directed the light to the left it reflected a dazzling array of bottles and a mirror placed between the two windows. I swept the light across the room. On the far wall was a fireplace with a big screen TV mounted above it. In front of it was a huge leather couch and a couple of chairs. To the left of the seating area, toward the back of the room was a pool table. I moved the light up and saw the walls held shadow boxes. Andy had said not to try and remove the jerseys they held as that might damage them. Instead, I was supposed to take them down and put them outside. If there was time, I'd signal Jake. He'd pull up and we'd slip as many as we could into the back seat. The smaller stuff, balls and cards, would go in the duffel bag.

A small creaking sound made me freeze. A dog? Was there a dog after all? No. I recognized that sound it just didn't quite register. Then I heard another sound. A choking sort of snort followed by a sonorous inhalation. It was the sound of someone snoring, only a few steps from where I stood. That familiar creaking sound had been the sound of leather as someone turned over. Someone was in here with me, hidden by the back of the leather couch they were sleeping on. The phrase, my blood froze in my veins, is a cliché for a reason.

At that moment, before my brain and body reconnected and I could take some kind of action, I heard a car pass through the otherwise silent neighborhood. A car with its music cranked to the max, bass thumping, voices screaming, windows probably open as someone drove through the richy rich neighborhood no doubt hoping to disturb the sleep of the one percent. I don't know if it woke anyone else, but it sure had that effect on my roomy. A person who had slept through the grinding sound of eight screws being torn from their place, a set of bars ripped away from a window, my footsteps across the hardwood floor. None of that had bothered him, but the thump of a loud stereo had. He woke with a start and sat up.

I saw his head and shoulders. His face a pale half-moon as he turned toward me. The dark circle of his mouth as he gasped with surprise and dove out of sight. I ran toward him; sure, he was going for a gun. Sure, that if I didn't get to him before he got to it I was a dead man.

The narrow beam of my flashlight bounced across a gun on a coffee table and a man wound in a sleeping bag, struggling to get free. I changed direction and ran for the window, jumped through and got tangled up in the step stool. I hit the ground hard, kicked my legs free, then sprinted for the car. I ripped open the door and jumped in. Jake was already turning the key.

"Go! Go!" I shouted under my breath.

He did, but not straight ahead, instead he spun the car into a hard U turn and took off down the hill and out of the neighborhood.

"One of his men was inside," I explained curtly.

I looked through the side view, ducking down so I could see Rose's driveway. A figure ran into the street. Then we turned a corner, and I couldn't see him anymore.

"Damn it. Damn it to hell." I said, chewing on my knuckle, an old habit I thought I'd lost.

Behind the wheel, Jake sat quietly, calmer than I was. Although he'd had a shot of adrenaline, it hadn't been the sustained hit I'd taken since hearing that creak of leather and knowing I wasn't alone. He didn't say anything though. Didn't ask any questions. Giving me time to wind down. He had driven us to park and ride and pulled in amongst a handful of cars. It was a parking lot for the use of commuters who rode the train. At this hour there were few using it, probably graveyard workers.

I wasn't concerned about the lack of cover. Even if Rose's men were out looking for us it was highly unlikely they'd find this particular parking lot. Besides, the car was as nondescript as you could get. In fact, one of the two other cars nearby was the same make and model, only white instead of blue. No, what bothered me was that the entire thing was over. I was not going to finish the mission. No money for Letitia. No help for Booker. Nathan's career over before it had begun. My short stint as a recovery agent, yeah, that's what I'd started calling myself, was over before it started. Laughably over.

"That was pathetic," I finally said.

"Stop it. You couldn't have guessed they'd have someone in there."

"Yeah, I should have."

"Because of Andy?"

"Yeah, and you're thinking the same thing."

"That Andy skulking around alerted them? Yes. When I put myself in their shoes—"

"The way we should have."

"The way we should have," he agreed.

"And if we were in their shoes we'd have been on high alert. We'd have maybe thought that Andy wasn't working alone, and we should keep an extra eye out."

"For a while."

"Which is what we should have done. Waited awhile. A couple weeks and they'd have probably decided it was a one off and gone back to business as usual."

"Only we didn't. So now what?"

"So now I guess we give up."

Jake stared at me with undisguised astonishment and then said, "Bobby Fucking Poe rolling over on his back. Never thought I'd see the day."

"Fuck you."

"Bobby Poe giving up and crawling away. Or should that be clucking away. Bawk, bawk, bawk."

"You sound like a five-year-old."

"You sound like a chicken. Bawk, bawk."

"Fucker. Bawk bawk yourself." I cracked up laughing and Jake joined me. We sat there, two grown ass men, laughing until tears ran down our cheeks, occasionally clucking at each other.

CHAPTER EIGHTEEN

The hospital kicked Andy loose as soon as they could. That government insurance doesn't make for long stays. Jake packed up some of his files, left his computer for us to use, rented a hospital bed and told Andy he'd be staying in the apartment next door to mine until he was better.

I got tires on Princess and got her running well enough that I could take Andy to his physical therapy appointments. It could have been a peaceful time, but it was anything but. Andy was obsessed with finding a way to take away all of Hugh Rose's sports collection. He spent hours on the computer reading every word and learning everything he could about both Roses.

In the meanwhile, I finished the '57 Chevy project and got the final payment. After that I worked on the

Coronet and contemplated whether it was time to find a burger flipping job, or to give Jake his bike and apartment back, take Princess and drive away. The three years I'd spent on the road had been pretty good ones. Sure, I'd be giving up seeing my old family and friends on the daily, but I'd make new friends.

It was around a month after the failed break in that Jake left for a weeklong book tour and I started to think seriously about renting a new storage shed and moving my stuff out of the apartment. I thought about how I'd just finished emptying out the old one, but that's how life works. I was sitting on the front porch, nursing a bottle of warm beer, and running through what I'd pack and what I'd leave, when Jake drove in. My energy was at an all-time low, so I just raised my beer in a lazy sort of salute.

"How'd it go?" I asked as he walked up.

"Decent. Hung out with a couple other thriller writers. I'll wait until I'm in some literate circle and drop names."

I nodded.

"Nothing? Not even a chuckle? Damn, you're a tough crowd. How's Andy?"

"He's good. Took the bus over to the halfway house to hang with some of his friends. I think you'll be getting your office back soon. Two more weeks of PT and he'll be done."

"It could have been worse," said Jake.

"A lot worse," I agreed. An image flashed through my mind of Andy laying on a table in a morgue instead of a bed in a hospital. I shook it off, but the dark coil of anger remained. A hungry thing lodged in my chest. "He's been researching the Roses'."

"Learn much?"

"Not really. About what we already got from Howie. Oliver runs the limo service part of the business. They use it to transport hot items, high-end car parts mostly and to take the girls here and there. Hugh is the one who runs the drugs and gambling. His nightclub is supposed to be legit, but he's got dealers in there. Howie figures they don't know Hugh is their supplier, just that he'll look the other way if you buy the right bottle now and then."

"Double dipping son-of-a-bitch ain't he?"

"You can't say he's stupid. Or that he doesn't protect himself or his stuff. There's been sort of a new development. He's hosting a special party at his house next month. Already talking about it to the papers according to Andy. There was an article about how he bought a new card for his collection. A rare, autographed Michael Jordan that, get this, last sold for two million dollars. The owner died and it came up for auction. They're saying he paid like two and a half."

"Two and a half million dollars?" Jake said and whistled. "That's crazy."

"Unless it's just a drop in the bucket to you."

We both thought about that for a moment. Then Jake said. "I wonder. If I had something that valuable sitting in my house maybe I wouldn't be paying so much attention to the other stuff I own. Maybe I'd be a little distracted showing it off to, well, whomever the hell I wanted to impress."

I found myself smiling. "Distracted, huh?"

"Yep. And surrounded by a crowd of people. Rich, important people you wouldn't want to knock down running to say, see what triggered an alarm."

Again, we were silent, contemplating the possibilities.

"It would be best if there was someone on the inside who could share a few things like for instance, where Hugh, Muscles and The Other Guy were."

"And how many rich people were between them and the door?"

"Yeah, something like that. I wonder if one of his people is hungry enough to be bought off. That maintenance guy might be a possibility."

"You think they'd invite the guy who cleans the pool and sweeps the driveway to this kind of thing?"

I shook my head. "Hell no. My brain fell out of gear for a minute."

"No doubt.

"You have a better idea?" I asked.

"I do."

"Yeah, what is it?"

Jake kicked the toe of his boot into the gravel, digging a small divot and staring down at it.

"What?"

He looked up, met my eyes, and said, "Zoey."

"Zoey? What do you mean, Zoey?"

"Look, I called her last night and—"

"Called her. You said she wasn't in touch. You said you didn't even know where she was or how to reach her."

Jake had the intelligence to lower his eyes and try to look ashamed.

"Okay, well I lied about that. You know how you two are. On again. Off again. She always leaves. You always get hurt. I was trying to protect you. I just wanted to—"

"Fuck you." I jumped to my feet and threw the bottle on the ground. It caught the edge of the sidewalk and shattered. It's true, breaking glass does get your attention on some atavistic level. I stared at the broken pieces. Then I looked at Jake. "I'd say I'm sorry for losing it but you know better than to fuck me around like that where she's concerned."

"I know. And honestly, I'm the one who's sorry. 'Mysterious love, uncertain treasure, Hast thou more of pain or pleasure! Endless torments dwell about thee: Yet who would live and live without thee!'" he quoted.

"Shakespeare?" I asked.

"Joseph Addison. Or maybe you'd be more familiar with, 'You made me cry, you told me lies. But I can't stand to say goodbye.'"

"Ozzy?"

"Nailed it," he said. "Got any more beer."

I did.

Jake laid out his plan and I didn't like any part of it and told him so.

He said, "I don't see any other way in." He rubbed his fists on his legs just above his knees. A sign of frustration. "Look, I know how these people think. People who can drop over two million on a sports card, they aren't like the rest of us."

"You can say that again."

He didn't. Instead, he said, "They have to show other people, not us, but people like them, that they've got money to burn. That's why he's inviting all these people to a party at his place, to show them this card he bought. It's proof he made it. A status symbol, like the women he surrounds himself with at his nightclub. You ever been there?"

"I have not and I'm a little surprised you have."

"Yeah, well I've got friends in low places and fans in high ones. One of them, a fan I mean, insisted on taking me there last year. He ordered the most expensive champagne in the place. It was delivered by one of the most beautiful women I've ever seen. Hugh Rose came over with another woman on his arm, who also looked like a model. I didn't know who he was at the time, and he didn't say his name, he just said, "Nice to meet you, I'm the owner. Hope everyone is treating you right. This is . . ." I don't remember what the woman's name was, but he introduced her and said she'd be around to help us with whatever we wanted. I wondered what whatever extended to, but you know, Cassanda would probably not appreciate my exploring that question."

"Probably not."

"Aside from showing off their toys, these rich guys love showing off women, beautiful women they probably wouldn't consider marrying or seriously dating. I did some research on the lifestyle for one of my books. These girls don't actually work for them. At least they don't usually get a paycheck. Instead, they get nice presents. They might be models or students, whatever, who enjoy the lifestyle of the rich and famous. They hang out with rich people. Fly on rich people's private planes. Visit private islands and resorts and houses they'd probably never see the inside of unless they were working there. That's why I thought of Zoey."

"That's a dick thing to say. These women sound like they're selling themselves to the highest bidder. Zoey isn't like that."

"No, she's not and I'm not saying she'd want to play that game but face it, she lived it. She married that rich asshole."

"But she didn't stay," I argued. Hating the idea that Zoey married for money and knowing the safety that money brings would have been enticing to someone with Zoey's childhood.

"Yes, she walked away. You helped her walk away and it cost you a year. So no, that's not Zoey, but she could play the role. She's got the face, the body and that special Zoey . . . Come on, you know what I mean."

Of course I did, and I didn't have to be a writer like him to describe it. I remember once, Zoey and me standing outside Lincoln Hall on the college campus.

She was shivering because she'd forgotten her jacket and refused to take mine. While we talked and shared a cigarette three different men and one woman stopped to offer her their coats. Each was rewarded with a soft thank you, an assurance she was going inside in a moment, and the full impact of those long-lashed, doe eyes. Each of them shot me a look that said exactly what kind of jerk I was to let her stand there in the cold.

Zoey had a certain fragility that demanded a protective response. I remember learning something in biology and wondered if it applied to her. It was how big-eyed kittens and puppies trigger humans to release the hormone oxytocin, which is associated with feelings of nurturing. I wasn't sure oxytocin was the reason she got that reaction, but it was as good an explanation as any.

"What I'm thinking is that Zoey can visit the club on a Saturday night, when we know Hugh will be there," Jake explained. "She'll make sure he sees her, and we both know he'll move on her. You gotta know that. When he does, she'll figure out a way to get him to invite her to the party. Maybe mention she saw it in the paper or something."

"I see you've been thinking a lot about this."

"Well, don't be pissed," he said, picking up on my mood. "You want to get even with him for what he let his men do to Andy, don't you? And she said she'd be willing. I laid it all out for her. She sounded kind of excited to come back for a visit anyway."

Jake didn't say more. Didn't try to convince me it was a fail proof plan. No, he just let me think about seeing Zoey again. He knew that would be enough.

He was right.

CHAPTER NINETEEN

Zoey's flight was supposed to leave Tegucigalpa, Honduras at 6:45 a.m. before stopping in San Pedro for a short layover. Then she'd gone on to Houston, Texas and then Las Vegas. After that final layover, she was heading to Portland Oregon. Her flight due to arrive at 11:55 p.m. was, of course, late.

I paced the halls, staring down at the distinctive carpeting. Thinking random thoughts like how so many of my friends took pictures of their feet standing on that carpet, then posted them on social media to announce they were traveling. That made me wonder if Andy's kind ever made use of that information. Something I'd have to ask him one day.

Time moved in that weird erratic way it can, slow as a geriatric sloth, fast as a Dodge Tomahawk superbike. Finally, the crackling speaker announced the arrival of her flight. I made my way to the area near her gate and stared into the milling crowd of passengers who had disembarked and were winding their way out to find their luggage.

I didn't recognize her for a moment. I'd been looking for a mature woman in her mid-twenties, elegant and stylishly dressed. The way she'd looked the last time I'd seen her, right before I'd pounded her husband into the ground.

Instead, she looked like a teenager. Her blond hair was swept back in a high ponytail. She wore a gray t-shirt, blue jeans, lime green sneakers. A big canvas bag with leather straps, the kind you see girls carry on the beach, was slung over her shoulder. Sunglasses were perched on her head. She was barely moving forward, letting the crowd push her along, as she scanned the waiting crowd. The Honduran sun had given her a light tan. She looked amazing. She looked like my Zoey.

I knew the moment when she saw me. She stopped and the crowd spilled ahead, moving around her. Leaving her behind. Then, she smiled and started walking again. I waited until she cleared the narrow opening in the half wall then moved in. She gave me a brief hug. So brief I didn't even have time to put my arms around her. It was awkward and amazing. Her hair smelled like sunshine. Is that a strange thing to think?

"Got luggage?" I asked inanely. She nodded and I gestured toward the sign with an arrow indicating the luggage carousel was downstairs. We took the stairs, and I was conscious of her nearness with each step.

"I've got two. The big one is a purple hard case with a Deadhead sticker and the little one is a fake Louis Vuitton."

"Fake."

"The monograms are cuss words."

"Sure."

"It's brown," she said, seeing my lost expression.

We found both fast and headed back up and then outside so we could cross the road to the parking structure. It was like stepping out of a dark theater into the light only reversed. The bright lights indoors made time irrelevant. Outside it was chilly and dark. Under a flickering streetlamp a group of three women speaking Italian stood talking under a no smoking sign, smoking like mad. I was pretty sure they could read the sign and didn't care. In fact, they probably thought Americans were insane for having all these rules. It wouldn't be the first time I'd heard that.

We moved deeper into the echoing parking area. "Row C," I said, for no real reason. I was in the lead.

"Bobby. Is that? Oh man, it is. That's Momma's old car. That's Princess." She sprinted past me and stopped to put her hand on the trunk, smoothing the sleek black finish much as I had when I'd first seen it. She looked up at me with such childish glee on her face. Happy memories of washing this car, turning the hose on each other, laughing like carefree maniacs flooded my mind.

I stood rooted to the ground afraid to move and be overcome by this emotion, but it was hopeless. Every part of me wanted to absorb her essence, to tase her lips, caress her skin, and feel my heart beating fast with the need of her. She looked into my eyes, and I could sense her desire for me, that deep sense of connection and longing that had always been there.

She stepped toward me, and I reached out without hesitation. Our bodies intertwined, her arms wrapping around my waist, mine enveloping her, pulling her close. I kissed her and time no longer moved fast of slow, it just stopped. All that mattered was the two of us and this moment. The concrete, the cars, the whole world faded away leaving nothing but the two of us and the intensity of our love for each other.

The drive to my place was filled with growing tension. Her hand on my leg was warm and the warmth grew to an uncomfortable level of heat. The scent of her familiar perfume, a blend of flowers and spice, filled the car and I found myself inhaling deeply. Every now and then, she would run her fingers down my face, touch the corner of my lips, or playfully tease me by pretending to unbutton my shirt. I warned her with a husky whisper that she was in danger of not making it to my apartment. That I might have to pull the car over.

"I always did love this car, Bobby," she purred back. "Don't you remember?"

I didn't say another word, just stomped on the gas and made record time. It was nearly three in the morning when I finally pulled into the carport. Ever the gentleman, thanks to Mrs. Sparrows teaching, I got out and hurried around to open Zoey's door. She was already getting out and shut the door behind her.

"I'll grab the luggage I said, twisting the key fob and looking for the unlock button.

"Fuck the luggage," she said.

Once inside I slammed the door shut and then pulled Zoey into my arms, desperate to feel every inch of her against me. I needed her and miraculously, she seemed to need me. We tore our clothes off in a frenzy that was both primal and all-consuming. With no patience to find a bed, we tumbled onto the couch like two hormone-driven teenagers. I slowed only enough to treasure the warmth and softness of her body as if it was the only thing on this earth that mattered. Maybe it was.

She pulled the band from her hair, and it fell loose, the silkiness of it entwined in my fingers. I reveled in the sensation. Then I began to kiss and lick every inch of her that I could reach, while my body ached with want. When I finally entered her, the sensations were so intense that I climaxed quickly, but it was only a fleeting moment of release. Almost immediately, I craved her again. I was driven to savor every moment, losing myself in her. Terrified she'd be gone again and forcing back the pain of that thought with the overwhelming force of my need.

Eventually we were spent, and she slipped into an exhausted sleep, the blanket she'd knit for Jake draped across our sweat slick bodies. I lay on my back while she lay on her side, stretched alongside me, her head on my shoulder. I was tired but didn't fall asleep until the first pale wash of light touched the windows.

I woke to the growling sound of the coffee machine and the smell of coffee. The thought of Zoey being there did the rest. I pushed the blanket away and sat up. Zoey stood in front of me, wearing my button-down blue shirt from the night before and holding out a steaming cup of coffee.

She rumpled her hair and yawned. "Shower then luggage, or luggage then shower?" she asked. Then she grabbed the edge of the shirt she was wearing and tugged it up a few inches. I reached for her, and she stepped back.

"Shower then?" She backed across the room toward the door to the back of the house and I took a cautious sip of coffee then got up to follow.

It was different this morning. Slower. In some ways better. We soaped and rinsed each other's bodies. I pulled her against me and felt her lips against my neck, then her teeth. I touched her in all the ways and all the places I knew she liked and was rewarded with a soft moan.

When she was ready, I lifted her off the ground and pressed her against the wall. She wrapped her legs around me and moved like a wild thing, her nails digging into my back, urging me to the rhythm she wanted.

Her growing need drove my own and we came together, a wild thrashing, animal climax it took long moments to recover from.

When our breathing finally slowed, we gently bathed each other again. When we were nearly done, I swept my thumbs across Zoey's perfect nipples and she wrapped her wet hand around my flaccid penis, bringing it quickly half erect. We both laughed. It had always been our habit to arouse each other after making love. It was a sort of promise for tomorrow, for an assured future that the two of us never really believed in.

"I'll get dressed and get your luggage," I said. "I'm supposed to pick you up at your hotel and take you to meet Jake at his place for lunch."

"That's a hotel I'll never see the inside of," she joked. Then she raised her face and we kissed, long and hard. "Should I tell Jake to cancel and get some of the money back?" she asked.

The question was really, did we want Jake to know that we were sleeping together? I wanted to shout it to the world, but did she?

"It's up to you," I told her.

She thought a moment and then said, "It's Jake. I'll tell him to save his money. It's not like he won't know anyway. We're both smiling like the cat that swallowed the canary."

"The canary? Never heard it called that before. Couldn't it be something bigger, like say, an ostrich?"

"Oh my god. Go get my luggage!"

CHAPTER TWENTY

I opened Zoey's door, and she climbed in. Moving with that unconscious grace that made something catch in my throat. Her hair was damp, and she smelled like a combination of my sage soap and her perfume. It was a good mix. She put on her seat belt and when she turned back toward me, I leaned in through the window and kissed her. I couldn't help myself. I put my hand on the back of her long neck and felt her skin soft and warm against my palm. I was tempted to unbuckle her seat belt and take her back inside.

She pulled away and looked up at me, a gleam in her eyes. "Get your ass in the car, Bobby Poe. We got work to do."

"But—"

"No butts or any other body part. Work.

"Fine," I said and laughed way harder than her joke deserved. I was happy and we had the whole night ahead of us.

Jake had asked us to come to his house around eleven while the rest were to show up at noon. That way he'd get some alone time to see Zoey. To Jake, Zoey was a sister just as surely as we were brothers. I stood in the background as they hugged, and Zoey oohed and aahed about Jake's house. He asked if she'd like a tour and I unglued myself from her side, reluctant as hell as he swept her away.

I busied myself with pouring us some coffee and refilling Jake's cup. The ubiquitous yellow legal pads were piled on the table. Getting it down on paper was Jake's thing. I sat down, pulled one toward me, grabbed a pen and started doodling.

I heard the back door open and Jake and Zoey's voices. Jake must have taken her out and through the backyard.

"I love your lawn," I heard her say. "Our grass is always sunburnt and kind of brown, but I'm not complaining. The house is fabulous. All stone with brick around the windows and doors. It was a vineyard and then a B&B and then a clinic. When they built the new clinic in town, we bought the house. We have almond, mango, papaya, and banana trees on the place and hydrangeas, which make me nostalgic every time I look at them. Remember the ones in front of Mamma Curtis's house?"

"Not really."

"Such a guy," she said, and her laughter, for once, didn't lift my spirits. We bought. Our yard." Who was this person she was sharing her life with? The idea of a life that didn't have me in it, that was thousands of miles away on a different continent was like a slap across the face. It woke me up to the reality that Zoey wasn't back, she was just visiting—a temporary. I felt something between loss and panic and suddenly the air was too thin. I couldn't breathe. I was gasping, drowning in the dark that was pressing in from all sides. I fell forward, saw the floor rushing up at me and then nothing.

I came to on the aptly named hardwood floor, Zoey was kneeling on one side of me and Jake on the other. Something cold and wet slid down my face. Was it tears? Mine? Zoey's? No, it was water dripping from the wet washcloth Zoey was wiping my forehead with.

I pushed her hand away and sat up. "What happened?"

"You passed out," said Jake.

I was grateful he didn't say fainted.

"Did you eat today?" he asked.

"No. I was in a hurry and Zoey said she just wanted coffee."

"His blood sugar drops if he doesn't eat," Jake explained to Zoey.

"He should have told me. I'd have made sure he had breakfast."

"I'm fine now I said," getting to my feet.

They made me sit and eat a bowl of cereal that Zoey sliced bananas into, insisting the fruit was healthier than just a bowl of sugar flakes. She was probably right. Of course, not eating hadn't made me pass out. It was my old friend the panic attack. Gasping for air and hyperventilating, expelling too much carbon dioxide I became confused, thinking I was back in that narrow cave. I fought even harder to breathe until my brain, short on blood and oxygen said enough and I lost consciousness. Passing out was not new to me. That didn't make it any less embarrassing.

I tried not to think about what had triggered it so of course it was all I could think about. Zoey and this other and the realization she was not here to stay. A knock on the door announced the next arrival and gave me something else to focus on.

Jake had tried to limit the invitations to people Zoey knew, Little Mikey, Heather, Letitia, Tilly but had added Andy because we needed his input.

Little Mikey joined me in eating a bowl of cereal, even though Jake promised lunch would be arriving soon. Tired of pizza, he'd ordered chicken pad thai and spring rolls. Letitia explained that Tilly couldn't come because, no matter what was going on, someone still had to run the business. While we waited for the food to arrive everyone talked over each other, hugged, and greeted Zoey, telling her how much they'd missed her.

I introduced her to Andy who shook her hand and said, "Wow. You used to date Bobby, huh?"

"Shocker, ain't it?" Jake said.

"Now stop that," said Heather, "It's true Zoey is pretty. I always think she looks like a cross between Natalie Portman and Kristen Bell. "Plus, she's got that gorgeous Rapunzel hair. So yeah, I guess some people would wonder why she liked Bobby, but once you get to know him—"

Everyone laughed at her unfiltered comment while she sat looking a little confused, but not unhappy. Heather was used to missing the occasional social cue and as long as the reaction was good she tended to shrug her shoulders and let it go. Which I was glad to see her do this time.

I looked around at the people seated at the table and realized how lucky I was. The idea of Zoey leaving was still there, a sharp blade waiting to impale my heart, but like Heather, I would let it go, at least for now.

Once most of the food was gone, we moved into Jake's living room to talk about more serious things. This time Andy started the conversation.

"First off, I want to apologize to Bobby. I messed up. The only reason they had that dude waiting for you was because my sneaking around warned them something might be happening. They were on high alert and that guy, who usually sleeps in the house, was in there and could have blown your head off."

"But he didn't and besides, Jake and I should have thought of it ourselves. It wasn't your fault."

"Well, it feels like my fault. From now on I promise I'll do what the crew wants. No more going off on my own. Okay?"

"Okay," I agreed, biting back a sarcastic response to his calling us a crew. We were no crew. We were a motley group of family and friends who didn't really know what the hell we were doing. I was going to fulfill the promise I'd made to help Letitia recover the value of her stolen weed. At the same time, I'd be helping Booker Robinson save his son from trouble. Even though that trouble was well-earned. Yep, I was going to be the hero of this story.

My new plan was even simpler than the old one. I'd wait until the party was in full swing. If I was lucky, I'd have someone, preferably Zoey, inside the house to let me know where Hugh, Muscles and The Other Guy were. Once I knew none of them were waiting inside, I'd blow the door, run in and grab what I could, then get the hell out. As Andy explained, there was always a lag in response time, and with the house full of people it would take a few precious moments for anyone to get outside and across the driveway to the building. Before they could, with a little luck, I'd have jumped into Jake's car, which he'd leave running this time, and we'd be gone.

It was Jake who laid it out for Zoey, "Once you're inside all you have to do is keep an eye on Rose and his two men. You'll have called Bobby before you went in, and you'll leave the line open. If it's safe to talk on your phone, you'll tell him where they are. If it's not, then you'll punch in a few numbers. He'll hear the beeps and know you're saying it's a good time to go."

"And how do I warn him if it's not a good time?" she asked.

"You don't have to. If he doesn't get a signal from you, he won't do anything."

"Really?" she asked, raising her eyebrows.

Jake looked at me and I nodded.

"Really," he told her. "Bobby's not quite the same hot head he used to be."

"I'm not sure my ex would buy that, but okay." She smiled at me, to show she was teasing. I smiled back, caught in her gaze. We must have held that look a little too long.

"Damn girl, I knew you were back," Letitia said to Zoey, but I didn't know *you* were back!" She made a gesture to encompass Zoey and myself. That's great. It's been a burden hitting on this man. Keeping those juices flowing for you."

"Thanks," said Zoey. "You were always the best kind of friend."

"You know it. But honest, he's been a trial. Glad you're back on the job, so to speak."

Both women cracked up and the group joined them, leaving me probably looking as confused as Heather had a moment ago. My confusion though didn't come from Letitia calling out the fact the Zoey and I were an us, but that I had no idea if that was true. I'd had no chance to ask her about what she thought us was.

I tuned back into the conversation to hear Zoey question whether Hugh Rose would find her attractive enough. It wasn't a fishing expedition. Zoey had always questioned her appeal. Not that she didn't know it was there. Life had demonstrated it to her in several ways. Dates. Modeling contracts. A rich husband.

However, she'd once shared with me that she thought her appeal had less to do with her looks and more to do with the aura she projected. "I think I put out an impression of helplessness, victimhood even. It must be irresistible to predators. The doe with the broken leg, or the lamb that's left the herd. All that lip-smacking and drooling isn't about me being hot. It's about me being defenseless."

At the time I'd told her she was wrong, that it really was her beauty that drew men like buzzards to roadkill. Possibly the worst idiom I've ever used. I told her that her theory was bullshit. That she really was that beautiful and she was definitely not defenseless. At the same time, I realized that she was looking at me, but that she was looking from a distance as if she were crouched in a hiding space somewhere far inside. It was a strange and somewhat disturbing impression. I shook it off. It was only my imagination running wild.

"Attractive enough?" said Heather, indignation in her tone. "With the clothes I've got planned. Oh my gosh you'll knock him dead. I was thinking that for the party you'd wear this little cocktail dress I designed. Wait until you see it. It's tight fitted with cute little cap sleeves and a sweetheart neckline, so not slutty at all, except the back is a deep V. Naughty, naughty. Oh, and it's in navy blue. I know, totally out of fashion, but on this dress it works and also I have a cushion cut sapphire and diamond necklace that will look insane with it. You'll wear your hair up so no one can miss it. Oh, and I think strappy stilettos. Something simple though, that won't draw attention away from the dress."

"Don't forget she'll need someplace to carry her phone," said Jake.

"Sure. I was thinking about this little beaded purse. It was a clutch but one of our craftspeople made a strap for it because I think holding a clutch all the time is annoying. Am I right, or am I right?"

I didn't know if she was right. I didn't know exactly what the hell a cap sleeve or a sweetheart neckline was either, but as long as Zoey and Heather knew what they were doing, it didn't matter.

"I'm going to steal Zoey for a while," Heather told me. "Oh, that's kind of funny. I'm going to steal her. You're gonna steal stuff. Anyway, I'm taking her to my store and she's going to try on clothes."

Zoey was sitting there with a bemused smile on her face. Heather in her element could be overwhelming. She seemed happy though, to be there, surrounded by her old family. Seeing that gave me a little bit of hope that maybe she would stay, that the "our" she'd mentioned was a harmless roommate or coworker and I'd jumped to the wrong conclusion. It wouldn't be the first time and probably not the last.

CHAPTER TWENTY-ONE

With Heather's promise that she'd drop Zoey off at my place later, I headed home not long after they'd left. But sitting at home, in the silence that suddenly felt empty, had me pacing the floor. I didn't want to talk to Andy or Jake, or anyone involved in our plan. I couldn't stomach going over it again, but the walls were closing in. I decided to call Howie.

"It's the shop. What you need?" he said with his usual greeting.

"You really at work? Kinda late, isn't it?"

"Bobby Fucking Poe. Yeah, but I'm here working on a side gig. Timing this damn Bronco for a friend but it's got no marks and—well hell, you don't care. What's up?"

"Nothing. Just bored and wondered if you wanted to meet and get a drink somewhere."

"Hell yeah. Same as last time?"

"Sure, be there in half an hour."

"Works for me."

I got to Murphy's Pub and Grill to find Howie had beaten me there and was already at his table.

"Bobby Fucking Poe," he said, his standard greeting for me. "How you been?"

"Been good," I told him, as I dragged a chair back and sat down.

There was already a beer in front of me and a plate of potato skins on the table They were steaming so must have just arrived.

"Help yourself," said Howie. Went ahead and ordered a beer for you too. Didn't want you to have to wait. You sounded thirsty on the phone."

"Right," I said, doubtfully but I still grabbed the beer and took a long swallow, so maybe he was psychic after all.

"What you been up to?" Howie asked and I filled him in on Zoey's arrival. I didn't mention our plans to rip off his boss's brother. He'd already tried to warn me away from Hugh Rose. Knowing I'd ignored his advice wouldn't make him happy. Instead, I talked about the Coronet and asked if he knew a good painter and someone who did upholstery.

"I do but they're expensive. You working?"

"I've picked up a few jobs here and there. Nothing solid yet."

"You'll find something soon," he assured me. "I've put out some feelers for you, but I've got nothing at the moment. Too bad you're not loaded."

"Tell me about it."

"I will. You know my boss?"

"I know of him," I said and shrugged, not wanting to seem too curious about the man whose brother I was planning to rip off.

"You asked me about his brother not long ago, remember? You had a friend that got ripped off. How did that end up by the way?"

"Unresolved. She's still hoping to get her stuff back but so far not so good."

"Sorry, man. Anyway, when I said wouldn't it be nice if you were loaded it made me think of something. My boss's brother just spent, get this, over two million dollars on a basketball card." He sat back waiting for me to be shocked or something. Of course, I wasn't. I knew all about it and wasn't a good enough actor to pull off looking surprised.

"I know," I told him. "Read about it in the paper. Michael Jordan, right?"

"That what I heard. Man, Oliver was pissed. He was yelling at someone in his office about it saying he didn't know his brother had that kind of money to throw away and they needed to talk about the redistribution of wealth and assets. Sounded like maybe it was his accountant in there, but I had to leave and never saw who it was. Pretty tense around the place the last couple of days. Bad enough when two business partners go at it, but when it's a family business?" Howie shook his head and looked worried. "Not sure how this is going to fall out."

"Could get ugly."

"Sure could. They never have got on well, but this is another level. Well, at least Gracey and Lacey are happy. You remember them?"

"How could I forget?"

"You couldn't."

"So, what are they happy about?" I asked.

"They're all excited about getting invited to a party Oliver's brother is throwing. Some kind of soiree just to show off a card he bought. He wanted pretty girls there, so he talked to Oliver and he's sending Lacey and Gracey. He even gave them a clothes allowance and I took them shopping yesterday. They had a blast."

"So, he's not sending them to the frozen north after all?"

"No, I think that's happening. He's been kind of holding it over their heads the last few months, but I think he might have given them the idea that if they do a good job at the party, he might change his mind. He won't. I know him too well. They've backed off the drinking, but they can't stop aging. I'd tell them, but what's the point? Let them enjoy the next few days. Those are some nice girls and I like them. Gonna suck to see them go."

We sat quietly for a moment, contemplating the fate of two sex workers who couldn't seem to break loose from the lifestyle. It was sad but while I sat there an idea began to form. Two women going to the party who had reason to hate their host. Me, needing someone inside to tell me to help keep an eye on him and his crew. As Zoey liked to say, the stars must be in the right alignment.

I had only been home for a few minutes when Heather and Zoey arrived. Both were loud and cheerful. They each carried bags and boxes which they dumped on the couch. A pair of high heels fell out of a box and slid to the floor. Zippered bags were more gently draped across the back of the couch. Once their hands were free both hugged me and enthused about how well their afternoon had worked out.

"We had a blast," said Zoey.

"She looks stunning. Just stunning," Heather said. Wait until you see. Zo, go put on the blue dress. Go on. Don't argue. You can surprise him with the lace, but he *has* to see the blue right now. I want to see his face."

"Yes boss," said Zoey. She shared a glance with me and hurried away.

"You should marry her," said Heather, after Zoey had left the living room, her arms filled with bags.

"Would if I could," I told her without hesitation.

"Then what's the problem."

"Zoey," I said, pointing my chin in her general direction. "I've asked her twice and she said no both times."

"But why," asked Heather, with the petulant whine of a child.

I shook my head. "I don't know. The first time, right after we finished high school, she said we were too young, and she wasn't ready to settle down. The second time, after I signed up for the Army, she said she wasn't going to sit around and wait for them to knock and tell her that her husband was dead. She didn't like me going in one bit."

"I see, I guess, but how about now? Maybe if you asked her now, she'd say yes."

"I don't know Heather. It's nice you think we belong together but...well I'll think about it."

"Well, don't think too long. Wait until you see her all dressed up." Her enthusiasm was returning. I didn't want to damp it down again by saying what Zoey wore didn't make a damn bit of difference to me. Heather's life was clothes, not mine. But then Zoey came back into the living room, and I thought maybe I could understand a little bit of Heather's perspective.

She hadn't had time to do much I thought. She'd only been gone a few minutes, and yet she looked completely different. Instead of an oversized band t-shirt and ripped jeans Zoey now wore a blue dress that showed off every curve and nuance of her incredible body. It was like a punch to the gut. The blue made her skin appear pale as milk. She'd pulled her hair into a bun, and I could see her long neck, her delicate features, the big brown eyes. Those eyes. She looked like a doll, like a brand-new Barbie doll dressed up and elegant, while I was GI Joe, left outside and found in the mud after a long winter. Heather had to see that the answer to why Zoey and I weren't together was obvious. She was way out of my league.

Heather stood with hands on hips surveying her work and then said, "Shoes?"

"I didn't bother with shoes," Zoey said. "My feet hurt enough from standing in your shop for hours. You should have seen her," she said to me. "I felt like I was modeling again, and she was a bully photographer."

"Wait until you show him the lace dress. Don't do it before the party though. I'm nervous he'll drag you off to his bedroom and we'll never see either of you again."

"Heather. You're scandalous as Letitia."

"Always was. Just not as noisy about it. Now, I better get out of here before Bobby kicks me out." She gave us each another quick hug. Heather was big on hugging. Then she took off.

I heard her car's tires roll through the gravel and still didn't move. I couldn't stop staring at Zoey, who was looking up at me with the most intense expression.

Was she feeling defenseless I wondered, as what she'd told me earlier popped into my mind. She was very slender, with fine bones and a certain air of fragility about her. But she was also tall and, I knew from experience, strong. The way she was looking at me made another thought enter my mind. The idea of a lion facing a fawn but just before it springs the fawn spouts spikes and fangs. Not exactly defenseless.

The look on her face told me that she wanted me, and the heat of her stare ignited a similar desire in me—and she knew it. My thoughts and feelings were a tangled mess. I wanted her in a physical way. But more, I wanted to talk to her, convince her to stay and be a part of my life. If she left again, it would be…it would feel like a part of me was dying, again. How could she keep doing this? I should make her sit down with me and tell me the truth about her life. Was there someone else? Someone serious. Hell, was she married? I needed answers but the truth was, I didn't really want to know the answers.

She reached up, and like a scene from a dirty movie, removed whatever was holding her hair up. It fell around her shoulders and she smiled and crooked one finger. I crossed the room in an instant. Cupping the back of her head, I drew her forward into a kiss. My teeth ground against her lips for a moment. She turned away, dropped her head to my chest and I brought my hands down and pulled her tight against me. The contours of our bodies fit so well it seemed as if they were melding.

This time I took the time to lead her to the bedroom, moving her toward the bed before slowly undressing her. I reached around her to unzip the dress and slide it from her shoulders. The entire thing dropped to the floor. I unhooked her bra and slid it from her arms, then hooked my thumbs in her panties and pulled them off. I stepped forward and she fell back onto the bed.

Taking time to remove my own clothes, even my boots, was out of the question. I unzipped my pants and pushed them down and climbed between her legs. She tried to say something, but I covered her mouth with my own. I didn't want to hear her words. The time for talk had passed.

At some point I did kick off my boots and peeled off of my clothes. I wanted to feel her skin against mine. I'd been needy and angry, and I still was, but I had burned off some of that anger in exertion.

Zoey had not fought my barely contained and violent mood. Instead, she matched my fury, biting and scratching until I felt my own blood slide down my rib cage. She brought blood-stained fingers to her mouth, licked one and used the others to wipe red lines across her cheeks like some tribal symbol. She laughed and I wanted to hit her, and fuck her, and love her. I did none of those. Instead, I rolled away and lay next to her, breathing her scent, absorbing her warmth as if she were the sun and I was a homeless man, freezing to death on a winter street. I slept.

When I woke up it was early morning. The dim light of the clock, which subtly cast the time on the ceiling and acted as a subtle night light was enough to see by. I could hear Zoey breathing and feel her weight on the bed. I got up carefully so as not to disturb her, then looked back at her. She was asleep on her stomach, naked. She was as close to the edge of the bed as she could be and not fall. One arm was draped over the side. Across her naked ass were the pink marks of my hands. Somewhere in our play, I'd spanked her. I knew it had been half in fun and half in anger. She reacted by moaning, tossing her head back and driving herself onto me. I spanked her again and again and saw her stop breathing, felt her shudder and felt myself respond. When she was done, she fell across my chest, making little sounds that made no sense and then I realized she was asleep.

I got up and stumbled across the clothes we'd left strewn across the floor. I softly closed the door then went to the bathroom to grab my robe before heading to the living room.

I was wide awake now and so spun up that if I hadn't been afraid of waking her up I'd have gone back for my clothes, got dressed, and went for a ride. It was the perfect time to get out there and watch the sun come up. Instead, I reheated a cup of yesterday's coffee and turned on the television.

Around seven, as I was playing a video game with the sound off, I heard the shower. Twenty minutes later Zoey entered the room, combing her damp hair with her fingers, already dressed in jeans and a Black Sabbath t-shirt. I was glad she was ready for the day. Last night had been wild. A little too wild. There were moments when I nearly lost control and could have hurt her.

Without saying a word, she walked over and sat on my lap. "Ouch," she said, "I think I have welts." Then she smiled. The kind of smile that told me she didn't mind and that she wasn't done with me yet.

"We, uh, we should get going," I said. "Supposed to go over things one more time, then rest up for tonight."

"I guess," she said, pouting. She got up, walked to the back of the couch, then reached forward until her palms were on the seat, her rump in the air. "What do you think? Is your couch the right height for this?"

It was.

CHAPTER TWENTY-TWO

After a wild night and morning of making love—no correct that—having sex with Zoey, I should have been happy. I was the opposite. That morning we'd moved right back into the rough stuff. I had a bandaged scratch across the Tasmanian Devil on my back and Zoey had a thumb-sized bruise on the edge of her jaw. These were not love marks so much as war wounds. The sex had been great. It always was. But in the past the connection between us, the love we had for each other always wound through the lust, making it more—I don't know—just more.

But last night and this morning I hadn't felt that same connection. I wanted it but instead, it had only seemed a little dangerous, a little desperate, and a whole lot like goodbye. Was that the problem? Had I decided she would be leaving me again and so I'd drawn away, hurt and angry?

I didn't actually know that Zoey planned to leave. I was inventing things, a worst-case scenario. Then, on the flip side, was my fear of her leaving totally unfounded or an excuse? I mean, in a way it was like that car you owned and loved that broke down and left you on the side of the road a few times. Even though you got it fixed. and odds were it would never happen again, you know you have to get rid of it. That you will never trust it.

Did I want to be done with Zoey? Did she want to be done with me? I wasn't sure I wanted to examine that too closely just yet. Besides, the reality was that I couldn't afford to think about anything too deeply right now. We were about to rob a career criminal. I had to stay focused. Letting myself get distracted would be the apex of stupidity. Andy had been hurt. I couldn't risk anyone else.

So, we went over it again, Jake, Zoey, and I. The plan had few moving parts, but it felt right to keep fine-tuning it anyway. For me, if for no other reason than to get out of my apartment and out of my head. Again, we had lunch at Jake's, but this time he cooked. No one wanted to call in an order and have some stranger come to the door. There was a weird vibe in the room. It was made up, I thought, of equal parts anticipation, impatience, and dread. We had set ourselves on this path and this was the time to back out, but it seemed we weren't going to.

After the meeting Zoey and I headed back to my place. We didn't talk much. Mostly Zoey spotted places she remembered and noted what looked the same and what had changed. A lot had changed. A frenzy of building that was both good and bad. The local economy was buzzing, but the influx of people was changing the landscape. The rolling green fields were quickly being replaced by mega apartment complexes and mini malls.

When we got to my place I grabbed a bottle of water from the fridge, sat down on the couch, and turned on the television. Zoey stretched, yawned, and said she was going to get her clothes ready for tonight. I think I replied but I'm not sure. The next thing I remember is waking up stretched out on the couch.

It was still light outside. I half sat up and looked around. Zoey was sleeping on the other section of the couch. The red blanket had been thrown across our legs. A sharing that healed a lot of the hurt I'd been feeling. I looked at the woman lying there, beautiful but even in sleep, her brow furrowed, her tension palpable as she fought through some nightmare. I wanted to go to her and hold her and promise that nothing and no one would ever hurt her again. I'd done that before, especially when she woke in the early hours, shaking and terrified. But it had been a lie. I couldn't protect her from the demons of her past. So instead, I watched over her and saw her move into a more peaceful place. As her breathing slowed, I was able to shut my eyes and join her in sleep.

The next time I woke it was dark out and Zoey was gone. I got up and wandered into the kitchen, where the microwave told me it was a few minutes after eight. Zoey stepped into the living room quietly, and then seeing I was up said, "I hope you're cooking something in there. I'm freaking starving."

She was wearing my bathrobe. The one Heather had bought for me, and a towel was wound around her head.

"Took a shower I see," I said with that brilliant insight only the half-awake can have.

"Yes, I did and so should you. Then you should make us something to eat."

"I thought that was your job."

"You really gonna go there?"

She pulled the towel off, then pretended to blot her hair dry as she moved toward me, a mischievous grin giving away her intent. When she got close enough, she whipped the towel back and tried to hit me with it. Luckily for me, I have combat training. Instead of running and exposing certain areas of my body as possible targets, I moved in and pinned her against the bar. She looked up, batted her eyelashes at me, and purred, "You'll never win that way, big fella," Then she tilted her head up and she was right, all the fight went right out of me, and I kissed her.

When the kiss was done, she sidestepped away, spun, and smacked me a good hard one with the towel. We were us again. I chased her across the kitchen and got the towel away from her. Disarming the enemy is important. We ended up with her standing in front of the sink facing away from me while I pressed against her and kissed and gently bit her neck and shoulder, concentrating on the soft, curved spot where they met.

"You are taking advantage of knowing my weak spots," she accused.

"Yep." She slid her hands down my forearms, brought my right hand up and kissed the scars on my palm. She knew my weak spots too.

I'd hidden the palm of my hand as best I could, but she'd seen the concentric scars. Scars earned by a hungry foster kid who needed to be taught that kitchens are not places for kids. That stoves are dangerous. "Once burned, twice shy," the old bitch had said, as she held my seven-year-old palm against the glowing red burner. Zoey knew where all my scars were. She liked to touch them and kiss them. She said she loved all of me and I should too. I guess her plan to make me accept myself was working. Now, when she kissed the cigarette burn scars across my shoulders or the corded bike chain scar across my lower back, I barely shuddered.

I took her hand and slid it down my stomach. She pulled away. "Oh no you don't. None of that. I have a party to go to and you have some cooking to do. Get with it, mister. I have to fix my hair."

I reluctantly let her go. The pain was manageable however, and in a short time I was humming as I placed spinach omelets on our plates and then covered them with salsa.

Zoey came out of the back of the house with her hair done. It was swept up in some fancy way with a few tendrils loose around her face. Artful disarray she called it. She still wore my robe. The combination was a killer. I swallowed hard, turned away, and poured coffee for us.

"Breakfast for dinner," she said and pulled out a seat at the bar. That looks amazing. Did I mention I wash stargling." Her words were somewhat muffled by a huge forkful of omelet.

After breakfast I obediently showered and then Zoey helped me put together an outfit suitable for a night of clubbing. An activity that was as alien to me as well, going out clubbing. Jake probably wouldn't be too proud of my skills with similes, but he was the writer, not me.

"Heather told me Fera Rosa Nightclub is divided in two parts," Zoey explained. "Upstairs is the dance area. They bring in DJs or live acts that attract a younger crowd. It's all big screens and laser lights and a lot of bass."

"Fera Rosa?"

"It's Latin for Wild Rose."

"They sure like their branding."

"They do. Now, the downstairs basement area is different. It's a VIP lounge. Bottle service, the whole deal. But unlike the upstairs, the downstairs is sedate. Music from below plays on speakers and big screens show the band and dancers upstairs. You basically get to see the crazy without getting sweaty and listen to the music without hearing damage."

"That sounds like something I'd like."

"Yeah, but it's not a place you'd be allowed into. I mean, this is where the pro basketball players and celebrities hang out. The only reason we're getting in is because—"

"Because of Jake, I know. It's so damn cold here in his shadow."

"Shut the hell up." Zoey laughed and threw an emery board she'd been using on her nails at me. Being a real man, I didn't even flinch.

CHAPTER TWENTY-THREE

When Jake arrived to pick us up the mood grew more serious. Since the time Rose's men had beaten Andy to now all we'd done is talk and plan. I was sick of both. I wanted to act and to hurt Hugh Rose. I also wanted to find a way to get back at Mitch Miller.

At first, I'd blamed Nathan for this mess. It had been his decision to gamble and therefore his consequences to pay. Then I'd learned how impossible they'd made it for the kid to pay back his debt. They were cheats and thieves with not a drop of honor. The only thing I wasn't sure about was what percentage of blame belonged to each of them. Were the decisions coming from Miller or Rose?

Jake parked at the rear of the building and handed his keys to a valet. Zoey took his arm, and I trailed behind. I was playing a not unfamiliar role. The friend without a date who'd been invited to come along.

We took the stairs down to the unmarked "special" entrance. The door opened onto a narrow corridor and two attentive bouncers. One was young with short dark hair, and a military posture. I thought, probably an off-duty cop. The other had a shaved head and an old scar across one eyebrow. For him, I guessed former boxer or cage fighter. They could have both been accountants who did serious workouts for all I knew.

After finding Jake's name on an iPad he carried the younger man indicated a door at the end of the hallway. "Thataway sir," he said.

Jake nodded and we headed thataway.

The VIP lounge was pretty much what I'd expected. A dim space with a bar running almost the full length of the back wall. The rest of the area was made up of sections, each section holding an L shaped couch, a couple of facing chairs and a plexiglass coffee table that glowed with a dim blue light.

Strategically placed screens high on the walls showed the dance area upstairs. Someone, or maybe a crew of someones, filmed the room, sweeping across the dancers and the DJ, zooming in on any action, someone tearing off his shirt, a particularly busty or dirty dancer. Even in this rarified atmosphere, sex seemed to be what sold.

As my eyes adjusted to the lack of light, I saw that the place was mostly blue and gold. Wallpaper with huge blue roses outlined in gold covered the walls. The trim was painted gold, and the doors were dark blue. We were led to our section, and I noticed the pillows on our white couch were either gold or a pattern of blue roses. Enough already.

A beautiful woman appeared at my elbow to take our order. Jake ordered a bottle of something I couldn't pronounce. I ordered a diet coke. I could read our servers thoughts. A rich guy out with his crass alcoholic friend who probably just got out of rehab. Only part right. Jake was the rich guy, but he was probably also the guy who should be in rehab.

We got our drinks and we waited. The crowd got bigger. At first there had only been a handful of people mostly quiet and barely noticeable in their own little corners of the room. I'd noticed the music was getting louder and the lights subtly dimmer. Murmured conversation was punctuated by laughter and shouted comments as the VIPs got more drinks in and lost some of their poise.

Zoey ordered a cheese plate. "Something to soak up the booze," she explained.

I should have been enjoying myself. The carefully crafted ambiance. The sound of an internationally famous DJ selecting the music and making sure it flowed seamlessly, matching the mood of the dancers, and keeping them on their feet and moving. The model level servers should have at least had my attention.

All I could see was Zoey, amazing, ethereal, the blue dress, white skin, a sparkle of sapphire, and those big dark eyes. Getting her involved in this was stupid. I found myself questioning Jake's foster family list. Sure, he helped us stay in touch and he often helped some of them—of us—but he he also asked for things. Things like asking Zoey to do this, or even asking me to help Leticia. I was sinking deep into blame and anger when the door opened, and a new feeling filled the room.

Hugh had come in, with Muscles right behind him. They went directly to the largest section in the center of the room. From here they had a 360-degree view. The moment the boss arrived the staff became more attentive, stood taller, smiled wider.

Jake and I exchanged looks but didn't say anything. We'd give them a few minutes to settle in. At Jake's nod Zoey began working the scene they'd acted out in rehearsals over the last two days. My role was simple. Sit quietly and look surprised.

"How dare you?" Zoey said in a low, throaty voice that nonetheless carried.

"Shut up," snapped Jake.

"Shut up? Zoey asked, as if she hadn't heard him right. "Did you—Did you. Just. Tell. Me. To. Shut. Up?" Each word was clipped and angry and each was louder than the one before. Heads turned toward us. I saw both Hugh Rose and Muscles staring. Perfect.

"Damn right," Jake said.

Even though I was expecting it, the wine thrown into Jake's face still startled me. Jake wiped his face clumsily, pretending a state of drunkenness I knew a few glasses of wine wouldn't have brought him to. "Why you miserable—"

I got up and stepped across the space, putting my arm on Jake's shoulder, and moving between him and Zoey. She got up and stood behind the couch as I got Jake on his feet and headed toward the exit. "Come on, bud, you had a little too much. Let's get you outta here. Get you home. Come on." I struggled with my not-so-drunk friend.

Once we were in the corridor, I told the bouncers the same thing. "Had too much. Gonna take him home." They let us by, and I half dragged, half carried Jake across the parking lot and to his car. "You sit here," It told him, "I've got your keys and I'm calling you an Uber. You sit here until it arrives."

Jake climbed in and seemed to behave. The next step was to go back in and head straight to the bar, leaving the road clear for Hugh Rose to approach Zoey. If he didn't, I'd rejoin her and we'd leave and try again another night.

I was relieved when the bouncers let me back in. I'd been a little worried they wouldn't without the presence of Jake, but it seems his celebrity status held even in his absence. Or maybe I just looked that damn good.

Zoey wasn't where I'd left her. I glanced around, trying for casual instead of looking directly toward Hugh Rose. It wouldn't have mattered. When I did look, he was gone along with his bodyguard. Maybe Zoey was in the lady's room. If so, she'd be back soon. No reason to get worried. Not yet. I scanned the crowd once again then sat and finished the diet soda I'd left on the table.

After a while I started to get worried. Where the hell was Zoey?

When a server drifted over, I asked if she'd seen my friend. She gave me a sympathetic look and bent close. "I think she left with a gentleman. She didn't have to tell me that "gentleman" was Hugh Rose. Her glance in the direction of his spot center stage told me that.

"Will your friend be coming back?" she asked.

I realized then that her sympathy was for Jake. The poor guy who had the wine thrown in his face and whose girlfriend left with someone else.

"No, he's going home. I'm sure they'll work it out."

"Of course."

I told her I didn't need anything else, and she went away while I sat there, trying to wrap my head around Zoey leaving with Hugh Rose. What the hell was she thinking?

CHAPTER TWENTY-FOUR

I found Jake sitting in his car waiting for us as we'd planned. I told him about Zoey, expecting him to be as anxious as I was.

"Guess it worked," was all he said. I'd never wanted to beat the shit out of him as much as I did at that moment.

The inside of the car felt claustrophobic, the smell of new leather and his fancy fucking aftershave made me want to puke. "You think she went with him to, what, to get close? To maybe . . ."

"Sleep with him? Hell no, you moron. You're talking about Zoey not some skank we hired off a street corner. You better hope she never hears you were thinking like that. She'd cut your heart out with her nails, and I'd sit and watch.

There wasn't much I could say to that, so I shut up. My phone chirped. I took it out of my pocket and saw a text from Zoey. *Gone dancing. See you at your place soon.*

I showed it to Jake. "What do you think she means by that?"

"I think she means she went dancing and will see you at your place soon."

"Damn it, Jake."

"We might as well get out of here. I'll drop you off so you can wait for her. You'll probably wear out the damn carpet but what can I do?" Seeing his try for humor had fallen flat he said, "Hey, don't be so down, our plan worked."

Jake was right, our plan had worked. Zoey had worked her magic and Hugh had fallen for the spell she wove. Just what I'd wanted, right?

Zoey showed up in the wee hours of the morning. I heard the doorbell and hurried to answer. I hadn't thought to give her a key. Didn't matter. It wasn't like her arrival would wake me. There was no way I could sleep. She came in bringing a hint of the night air, expensive booze, and perfumed girl sweat. Her hair was down and a little disheveled and she was barefoot, her shoes dangling from her fingers.

"Woo," she said, squinting against the light and bumping her hip against the doorway as she walked in. "What a night."

"What happened?" I asked. "I thought the plan was I'd come back in, hang at the bar, and watch to see if Rose hit on you."

"Yeah, well you weren't fast enough." Zoey dropped her shoes by the door and set her purse on the kitchen island. "I need water," she said and walked in that overly careful walk of the inebriated to the sink where she filled a glass with tap water.

"So, what happened?" I asked.

She turned toward me, sipped the water, and then said, "The minute you and Jake left; Hugh moved in. He told me he'd seen the whole thing and he was sorry my friend had caused a commotion."

"But you were the one who threw the drink."

"Well, yeah but I threw it at Jake and I'm prettier."

"You're also a little drunk, I think."

"Can't argue with you there," she said tipping the glass of water towards me and spilling a little in the process. "Can't nurse a drink forever you know. Anyhoo it's all fixed. I'm going to his place for lunch tomorrow. But right now, I gotta brush my teeth and pee, maybe not in that order."

"It might not hurt if you took a shower."

"Always the gentleman," she said. "Help me with my zipper." She turned her back and I unzipped her, then helped her take the dress off. I draped it over the back of the couch, and she gave me a little pat on the shoulder as she walked by, still sipping the water and swaying a little as she carefully made her way toward the back of the apartment. After a moment I heard the shower and her surprising alto as she belted out a song I couldn't quite make out. Something she'd heard at the club or maybe the last thing she'd heard in the Uber that brought her home I guessed.

Home. Was that here or was that the big stone and brick place in Honduras she'd told Jake about? I'd have to ask her that question soon, even if I didn't want to know the answer.

I heard the shower turn off and waited awhile but she didn't come back into the living room. I went to check on her and found her sprawled across my bed, naked, wet, and gorgeous. I flipped the bedspread over her and left to find my own bed on the couch. She was right, I was a gentleman, damn it to hell.

I flopped onto the couch and turned on the television, trying to replace the sight of her with the flickering scenes in front of me. I knew I might as well give up on sleeping. I'd be up all night. That was my last thought.

I was up before Zoey, making pancakes and thinking about how to approach the question that had come up again last night. Where was Zoey planning to make her home? I heard her moving around, the sound of the shower. No singing this time. Probably a world-class hangover. I poured us each a glass of pulpy orange juice thinking vitamin C could help. But when she burst into the living room she was wide-eyed and healthy looking.

"I smell bacon," she said, giving me a huge smile. "I love bacon."

“I know,” I said, smiling at her enthusiasm. “Made you pancakes too.”

“Oh boy, you win. I’ll do any deviant thing you want. Just make me pancakes and bacon. Only we’ll have to postpone the deviance. I phoned Heather. She’s on the way over to help me get ready for my date.”

My mood changed in a heartbeat. “How’s that going to work?”

“I’m supposed to meet him at his house.”

“What?”

“Easy there, it’s no big deal. He’s got a cook and he’s going to make us lunch.”

“He can’t take you to lunch somewhere?”

“He said he goes out a lot so having lunch at home is more special. Besides, he said we wouldn’t be alone. He has staff.”

“He said staff?”

“He did,” she said, laughing, either at Hugh Rose’s conceit or my concern. “Men,” she said, confirming my suspicion that it might be both.

Heather arrived and Little Mikey was with her. "Hey," I said, enthused at the prospect of having someone around who might want to discuss something not wardrobe related. "What are you doing here?" I asked him, my usual lack of diplomacy on full display. It was Heather who answered.

"When we got up this morning and it turned out Mike didn't have a job lined up, he decided to come with me and hang out with us."

I must have looked confused.

"Yes, Bobby Fucking Poe, catch a clue. Me and Mike have been living together for like what, she looked up at Little Mikey, "Six months or so?"

"Yeah, about that."

"But nobody said. I mean Jake and I always . . ." I didn't finish the thought. That Jake and I had always thought Heather was asexual and Little Mikey's crush a hopeless dream.

"Not everyone is into public display," Heather told me. "The world has plenty of Letitia's who like to put on a show. Me and Mike like to keep ourselves to ourselves. Don't we, babe?"

"That's right," he said, but he put one arm around her possessively signaling very publicly that the two of them were together.

"Jake's going to be blown away," I said.

"Uh huh, well, you'll both get over it," she said, obviously aware of the flawed idea we'd held about her.

Luckily Zoey, who had gone to the bedroom to finish dressing, chose that moment to walk in. The two women started to talk, and Little Mikey and I might as well have become invisible. I was okay with that.

The girls disappeared into the backrooms, popping out now and then to get our opinion on different things. Hair up or down? Definitely down. A summer dress or form-fitting jeans and a tank top? Tight jeans the winner. After that one Mikey and I snuck out to the relative safety of the carport.

Eventually, Zoey called an Uber, which arrived way too fast. I watched anxiously as the blue Prius pulled away, taking Zoey to have lunch with, as Andy would say, a bad dude. A very bad dude.

Mikey and Heather took off right after and as soon as they were gone, I got on my bike and headed toward

Arlington Heights. Was I going to change the plan and go keep an eye on Zoey? Hell yes.

Again, I conceded that there was no way to really keep an eye on the place, not without a damn drone. I did manage to drive by twice. There were no gunshots, no screams, no Zoey running from the house. I finally admitted defeat and went home to wait.

I didn't have to wait long. From the time she left to the time she returned a little less than two hours passed. When she got back, she was sparkling with enthusiasm and ideas to improve our smash-and-grab scenario.

"I have a lot to tell you, she said, "but first, let's go to bed."

Although I wanted to hear what she'd discovered I neither argued nor complained. I'm good like that.

CHAPTER TWENTY-FIVE

The day of the party was surreal. Everyone knew the plan, and everyone seemed like me, to be both dreading the ticking of the clock and wishing it would go faster. Hugh was going to send a car to pick Zoey up at her hotel at seven thirty. She and Heather would be there by six to prepare. In the meanwhile, there were a lot of hours to fill.

When we got up neither of us was in the mood for breakfast. "There's a park nearby. You want to go for a walk?" I asked.

"That would be great."

She was right. It was. The park was a long narrow greenspace that stretched between neighborhoods. It was mostly used early in the morning or late afternoon by dog walkers. At this time of day, when most people were at work, we had it to ourselves.

There was a wide dirt trail between trees and brush planted to obscure the view of houses and stores. It was effective. There was a sense that we were in the country, alone except for the birds and squirrels. After a while we noticed a shallow creek trickling along on our left. It got bigger as we went, widening in places, then narrowing again. Sometimes there was a wooden bridge. They, and the occasional bench or a garbage can chained to a post, were the only signs of civilization.

We held hands as we walked. The quiet was only disturbed by bird calls and in the far distance the sound of tires on asphalt, horns, and sirens. It was easy to shut them out.

At some point we came across a cluster of purple flowers. Zoey let go of my hand and clambered down a bank to admire them. "I think these are wild iris. Aren't they gorgeous?" she asked. She took out her phone and shot pictures.

This was the Zoey I knew best. Her passion for the flowers reminded me of the time we ditched school and rode our bikes to the beach. I got to watch her face the first time she saw the ocean. I'll never forget it. After that we walked along the beach. The breeze played through her hair and her cheeks got a little pink from the sun. Aside from the waves it was calm and peaceful.

Zoey was looking down, saw something, bent down to grab it. There was this look of radiant joy as she held it up for me to see. An intact sand dollar, like a treasure on the palm of her hand. The same look she'd worn when she saw the ocean. The same look, sometimes, when she saw me. In that moment my heart shattered.

I call that image Zoey light. Zoey dark is barbed anxiety, thrashing night terrors, and crippling self-doubt. I like Zoey light the best. If she'd let me, I'd make it my life's mission to make sure the darkness went away forever.

When we returned to my place we were both in a better mood than when we'd left. Zoey even admitted she'd woke up with a hangover but had decided to deny it away.

"It didn't work. Let's go find something to eat. Didn't Jake say we should come over for lunch?"

"He did. You don't mind hanging out over there?"

"Beats sitting here and counting every moment."

"I guess. Though we could entertain ourselves."

"We've had enough "entertainment," she said, drawing air quotes around the word. "Let's go see what Jake and Cass are up to. Maybe play some Yahtzee," she said, referring to our favorite childhood game.

"Right. Yahtzee. I can't wait." I tried to be upbeat, but Zoey was right. I *was* counting every moment, and in my imagination the ticking of that clock felt like a countdown to the end of the world.

I remember the sky was hazy that morning. The sun feeble behind it. I knew by noon that marine fog would burn off and the sun would be out in force, but for the moment the gloominess fit my mood. At Jake and Cassandra's house we learned Jake was by himself.

"Cass is out of town again," Jake told us. "She had to attend a friend's baby shower in the Dalles. Normally she'd have driven back home but I asked her to stay the night, so she found a hotel."

I thought, well at least Jake got lucky. She must really love him to put up with him and us and all the crazy.

By noon everyone showed up to touch base. First, Little Mikey and Heather, then Andy, then Booker and Nate Robinson and finally Letitia and Tilly.

There was something claustrophobic about being inside, so we ended up in Jake's backyard, sitting on lawn chairs on the wide stone patio, passing a bag of Lay's Original potato chips and a joint Tilly started. Around us was a golf-green lawn bordered by trees and flowering bushes, all contained within a six-foot-tall cedar fence. Although I knew there were neighbors the backyard felt cut off, an island of its own. It had a similar vibe to our walk in the park earlier, but there was more tension in the air. Eventually Heather said, "It's too quiet. This feels like a funeral."

"Mine, I guess," said Zoey.

"At least you'll be dressed for it," said Heather.

The bad joke eased the building tension and we all laughed, probably too long and too loud but that was okay.

"What are you going to do with all your vast wealth after this job?" Mikey asked me.

"I don't know," I told him honestly. "Finish fixing up the car, buy a bike, maybe get some decent tools."

"Hey. Those are fine tools."

"Just giving you a bad time."

"You leave Mikey alone," said Heather, "I'm the only one gets to give him a bad time."

"Well, that doesn't seem fair. That seem fair to anyone?"

Everyone agreed it did not.

"The house sold," said Booker. His deep voice resonated across the space.

Nate made a sour face but said nothing. I thought, he must have finally accepted this as part of the cost for his bad judgement.

"That fast?" said Zoey. "That's amazing."

"Yep. Took three days and we got more than asking. Market is hot, hot, hot right now."

"And it's a fantastic house in a great neighborhood," said Jake. "Looking forward to moving down by the river?"

"You mean living in a van, down by the river?" he asked, giving possibly the worst impression of Comedian Chris Farley I'd ever heard. "I was," he continued after the moans died down, "but I was giving it some thought on the way here." He looked at Nate and I realized whatever he was about to say was news to his son. "I'm thinking Nate's going off to college. Why do I want to be bumping around an empty apartment? I've got friends and family all over the country, the world even. I qualified for retirement two years ago. The apartment allows me to sublet. Why not put my stuff in storage, rent the apartment out and get the hell out of Dodge."

"Where would you go, Dad," Nate asked. I thought I heard a trace of anxiety in his voice.

"Oh, nowhere far. Not until you get settled at least. Hell, maybe even find a place near your school for a little while. Then, I don't know. Got a good friend up in

Massachusetts. He says the fishing is something out there. Keeps trying to get me to come up and stay with him. His wife passed last year, and I think he'd welcome the company. Got another friend in Hawaii and then of course there's my brother and his family in San Diego and my sister who moved to London and married a guy from there. I've never seen their daughter. Yeah, when I think about it there's a lot of places and a lot of folks I'd like to see. What you think Nate, that sound like a plan?"

Nate nodded. "I think that would be great."

Good, the kid seemed to have grown up a little through all this. I hadn't known him long, but the hot-headed responses were gone. This was a kid who had maybe learned to stop and think before he spoke, a good change. But then, what the hell did I know about kids? The foster kids I'd grown up with were all dealing with a tragedy of some sort, absent, even dead, abusive, alcoholic or addicted parents. A sense of not being wanted. Were other kids, normal kids from normal families, so full of self-loathing, depression, and rage? Could be. Maybe it was not a Mr. Roger's world for most. But at least with Nate there were signs that he'd survive being a teenager and end up as a decent adult. It was about all a person could ask, I figured.

"Tish and I are going to make some changes too," said Tilly.

I was a little surprised that she had spoken. It was usually Letitia who took the lead. Also, I'd never heard anyone call Letitia Tish before. Tish and Tilly. I almost said something, but I like my junk too much.

"What kind of changes?" asked Jake.

"We are for sure getting out of the marijuana business." She looked at Letitia as if for confirmation. Letitia nodded, then said."

"That's right. Now that the state is running the industry—"

"Let me guess," said Jake, "Too much competition. Too little profit?"

"What. Hell no. Demand is high. Prices are good. You think I can't compete with Uncle Sam? Oh please." She waved her hand in his direction as if he were an annoying fly she was trying to deal with. "No, it's just that I found a new opportunity. A friend of mine has a microbrew in Portland. They make the best beer on the planet, and they are growing like crazy. He wants to start a new line and to do that he needs hops, a certain kind of hops, grown in a certain kind of soil."

"Soil?" I said, as if I were dim.

"Uh-huh. Heavy mineral content, volcanic rock. They are thinking about using that in the name, Lava on the label, or something. He'll figure it out. Anyway, I found some land down south and—"

"South like Alabama south?" I asked.

"No, you dumb ass. Southern Oregon. I bought a place down there. It's got a big old farmhouse and a great barn. Half my crew wants to move down there with me. We'll plant the hops, but we'll also put in a big vegetable garden. The place is right on a main artery and already has a fruit stand on it. They were selling apples and lavender and what not, and I plan to expand on that."

Letitia's face was alight with excitement at the prospect of a new enterprise. The woman loved business as much as I loved Zoey. Well, probably not as much, but damn close.

"You know," Booker was saying, "There's not a lot of dark folks down in that part of the state."

"I know. I'm counting on me being a draw."

"That's . . . I don't know what that is," he said.

"That's Tisha," I said.

Being tackled and then rolled across a grassy lawn by a beautiful woman is much more painful than you'd think.

CHAPTER TWENTY-SIX

The clock had ticked its last tock. I drove Zoey to the hotel where Jake had registered her before she arrived and luckily, or lazily, never cancelled. There were a couple hours to go but Heather was going to meet her. Apparently, this occasion required the efforts of two women. I didn't love the idea that they were going to spend all that time making sure Zoey was the perfect date for Hugh Rose's brag party.

"Don't bother getting out," Zoey told me as I pulled up to the curb. "All I have is this," she said, indicating the zippered bag that held her dress. "You don't need to carry it for me. I'll see you tonight, on the other side of all this."

"I have so many things I want to ask you. Things I need—"

"I know," she said, stopping me before I could say more. "We'll talk tonight. Okay?"

I wanted to say no. No, I can't wait any longer. I need to know if we have a future. But I didn't say it because it wasn't true. I *could* wait. I *wanted* to wait. Because a part of me was afraid I already knew the answer.

She got out of the car and all she left behind was the scent of her and an emptiness in the pit of my stomach. Part of it was fear for her, but part was an old friend who liked to hang around when she was not there. A sort of sad companion.

I put the car in gear and pulled away keeping my eyes on the road and definitely not in the rearview.

CHAPTER TWENTY-SEVEN

I was pacing around Jake's living room when his phone rang. He picked it up and I heard him say, "Okay, I'll let him know. Uh huh. Right. Thanks." Then he hung up and said, "That was Heather. The car came for Zoey and she's on her way. We should wait," he looked down at his bare wrist, looking for a watch that had long been replaced by a cell phone. "We should wait at least an hour, don't you think?"

I didn't think, but I nodded anyway.

Forty-five minutes later, either because he couldn't stand my pacing, or because his own internal alarms were going off, Jake led us to the garage where we got into the old Toyota with its "special" plates and we headed for Arlington Heights.

It was dark outside. The moon, a tiny sliver in the distant sky, kept disappearing behind racing black clouds. The smell of rain was in the air and a sort of ozone smell as well. I thought it might be lightning burning somewhere close. There were heavy gusts of wind that bent the trees lining the road and made the phone wires swing. Everything felt erratic and charged.

We drove by Hugh's house. Lights were on inside, spilling gold rectangles across the lawn and circular drive, which was choked with cars, as was the narrow road. I guessed the neighbors weren't fans of Hugh's parties.

We had to find a place to park that was out of sight but near enough that we could react quickly to Zoey's signal. Jake had to drive three blocks before he found a spot but if we followed the rules, it was facing us the wrong way.

Jake said, "We don't want to stick out but don't worry, this baby can flip on a dime." He patted the dash and gave me a smile meant to inspire confidence. It didn't.

I took off my seat belt, then slumped down into my seat. I closed my eyes but the sense of waiting, and the dark brought me quickly back to a memory of suffocating sand and terror. I opened my eyes and stared down the street instead, counting the porch lights, the cars, distracting myself.

When my cell phone beeped, we both jumped a little. The small sound was like a live wire running down my spine. I grabbed the phone off the dash and looked at the succinct text Zoey had sent.

"2 bodyguards upstairs cook in kitchen two catering staff think that's all."

I had asked her to let me know where the employees were. I wanted the bodyguards as far away as possible, so I'd have time to hit the place and get out. If they were upstairs when the alarm went off it would take them time to get down the stairs, through the company, and out the door.

I looked at Jake and said, "I think it's time to go." I could feel the insane smile that I was wearing and the eagerness that was starting to course through me.

Jake and I were both wearing our wigs, the long hair tied into ponytails to keep them out of our eyes.

Now we put on our masks, quickly hooking the elastic behind our ears. Jake was as eager to get moving as I was. Nevertheless, after he started the car he pulled slowly from the space, making a U-turn without chirping his wheels or giving any other indication we were in a hurry. He double parked beside a black Tesla someone had left part way across the driveway entrance on the side nearest the building that was our target.

I carried a smaller bag this time. After all, I didn't plan to carry anything away with me. This operation had gone from smash and grab to distract and destroy.

I knew the door had an alarm, so I left it alone and moved toward the same window I'd worked on before. The sound of shattering glass was sure to get attention, so I didn't break any. Instead, I reached through the bars and used a glass cutter to scribe a circle. Then, using a gloved fist, I punched the circle, which snapped free, fell inside the building, and hit the carpeted floor with barely a sound.

From the bag I took the first of three large Mason jars. I loosened the lid then slipped the jar through the hole in the glass and heard it land with a thump followed by a pleasing sloshing sound. I did the same with the next jar. The third jar was special. It contained sodium chlorate, which I'd carefully made myself using a formula given to me by Kirk, the munitions guy who had taught me a thing or two before being killed. When the sodium chlorate hit the carpet, which would by now be saturated with sulfuric acid from the two jars I'd pushed through the window, the reaction should be powerful and effective. At least if a blazing fire was your aim. I heard the satisfying whomp of ignition and saw flames racing across the floor. My signal to go.

I jogged to the car and slipped in. This time, instead of a fast U-turn and a quick retreat, Jake revved the car. From the deep thrum, I realized it was not your run-of-the-mill Corolla. I should have known he'd long ago fixed up his old college ride.

Spinning the wheels, leaving tread, and making as much noise as a small car with sixteen-inch tires could, Jake did his best to call attention to the fact that someone had come calling. Once someone got outside and saw the flames casting their own special kind of light across the lawn they would guess that something bad was happening. Maybe Hugh Rose would eventually put together the loss of his stuff and the beating his men had given Andy, but I doubted it. Karma wasn't probably in his dictionary.

As we reached the bottom of the hill, I saw headlights coming up behind us over the top. I was surprised. I'd expected them to help try to put out the fire before coming after us but there they were, and they were coming fast. There had to be at least one, but probably two men in that car. That meant less for Zoey to be concerned with. That was a good thing. Now we just had to make sure they followed us—but didn't catch us.

The Hoyt Arboretum is one hundred and ninety acres of trees and trails, lots of trails. Pick the one we wanted and run like hell was the strategy. Let whoever was following try and guess which one we'd taken. It was a lot like hiding in a maze if the maze were pitch black, and full of tripping hazards.

Days earlier we'd mapped out which parking lot, the one near the zoo, and which trail, the one that lead north, back in the direction we'd come from.

Jake drove the little car into the lot at high speed and performed a little slide maneuver into a parking spot. We bailed out, heading for the trail. As we ran, I took off the mask and wig and shoved them in a pocket. Jake did the same and now we were two joggers out for a run—in the dark. Well, we were dedicated.

A jagged branch I hadn't seen slapped me across the face. I faltered but kept going. Soon after that I heard a rock rolling away and Jake stumbled. He managed not to fall but as we ran he'd let out a gasp now and then and I knew he was in pain. We slowed down.

I heard running feet behind us. Two sets, and they were closing fast. Grabbing a handful of Jake's shirt sleeve I pulled him off the trail and into a shallow dip in the ground under a pine tree. The tree's branches nearly touched the ground and concealed us. Hidden in the real shadows I fought off the imaginary ones.

We heard more than saw the two men run past and waited. A few minutes later the running steps came back, moving more slowly now. Their pace nearly a walk. "We'll never find him in here," one of them said. They didn't know there were two of us, which meant they didn't know much.

I heard their car start and was pretty sure they'd left, but we waited some more, just to be sure. Then, I walked, and Jake limped back to the trail and toward the neighborhood we'd been aiming for. He had twisted his ankle but he could still walk on it, more or less.

I breathed a sigh of relief when I saw Princess, black and gleaming under the streetlight where I'd left her. I opened the passenger door and watched Jake grimace as he got in.

'That was better than getting stoned," he said unexpectedly.

I wasn't ready to agree. Zoey was still back there, at that house with Hugh. I wouldn't be able to celebrate, or even take a deep breath, until she was home and safe.

CHAPTER TWENTY-EIGHT

Zoey arrived without ceremony in a black sedan that sped away before she reached the door. The fancy clothes were gone. She didn't even have the bag she'd carried them in with her. Instead, she was dressed in her torn jeans, a gray t-shirt and white converse. She'd never looked better.

She hugged me, there on the porch. The sense of relief that she was back, and safe, made me hold her maybe a little too tight.

"Gotta breathe," she gasped and pushed out of my arms, but she was smiling as she did it.

"Tell me everything," I said, as we went inside.

"Feed me and I will," she promised. "I'm starving."

"I thought this was a dinner party."

"So did I, but I was too nervous to eat and then there was this robbery."

We both laughed.

"I made spaghetti sauce," I told her. "Just have to boil some noodles. You still like those bowtie shaped ones?"

"Farfalle? You bet. Only they aren't bowties, their butterflies."

"Butterflies. Bowties. Potato. Tomato."

"I don't think you're saying that right."

I turned away to reach into the cabinet to get the pasta I'd bought knowing she liked it and to stop the strong impulse to reach for her again.

While I cooked, Zoey opened the fridge and took out ingredients for a green salad. We worked together like an old married couple. Not saying much but experiencing—at least I did—a feeling of compatibility. A calm and comfort that I rarely felt with anyone else.

I wanted to look at her while we ate so I dragged one of the stools into the kitchen. I poured a glass of red wine for her and grabbed a beer for me.

Then, we sat down opposite each other. I picked up my fork and said, "Okay, now tell me everything."

An hour later, empty dinner plates left for the morning, wine and beer moved into the living room, we were still talking. Only we'd moved on from the night's events to broader topics. We were both slightly drunk and in that odd sort of mood that sometimes happens after an exciting and dangerous event. There was a sense of relief but also a sort of letdown.

I'd been complaining about not having much. Told Zoey about my thoughts when I got out of jail. How little I owned and how much I owed Jake.

"Jake again. I'm so sick of hearing about Jake," she said, and I was surprised by the tight and angry tone of her voice. "So, what if he's loaded and some sort of benefactor? You'd do the same if you had his money. He's no better than you. In fact, if anything, you're like twins. Two peas in a twisted pod. You both have a thing about family. You both lost yours and you both have tried to make your foster family as relevant as your own."

"So, what's wrong with that?"

"Nothing. I think it's sweet. What I don't like is how you have it in your head that Jake's the one who does all the work."

"Because he does," I said, exasperated. "He keeps up on where everyone is and what they're doing. He's how I found you in California."

"Yes, all well and good. I'm not saying he's not a good person. I'm just trying to show you that he isn't doing it alone. I'm so sick of you elevating him while you put yourself down. Maybe he is the one who keeps everyone together, but who comes to the rescue? Who fixes things when it all goes wrong?" You do. You're the one who came up with the plan to help Letitia. All Jake did was ask for your help."

"But he was the one who offered to find her help. He also bankrolled everything."

"Yes, I get it. I agreed he is generous with his money, but he wouldn't be if he was dead. How many times did you stop him from killing himself. Twice that I know of. Is he still the way he was? Does he still go to that dark place?"

I looked away but that was answer enough.

"Oh Bobby, I'm not trying to be a bitch, even if I am a little drunk and tired and in a weird mood tonight. I just want you to value yourself. When things get tough for him, Jake gives up. When things get tough for you, you get tougher. I'm not saying he's not a brilliant, creative man. I'm saying, he'd never have got where he is without you."

She stood up, took two steps toward me, and climbed into my lap. She wrapped her arms around my neck, breathed against my ear. "Make me shut up Bobby Poe. Take me to bed."

I carried her to bed, but we didn't sleep, not for a long time. We were, for the most part, gentle with each other. Slow one moment, desperate and driving the next. The alcohol in our blood made us languid and relaxed but knowing this might be goodbye made me focus on every moment, savoring everything as if it were the last time we would be together.

At some point she validated my feelings. We lay there, catching our breath, her leg thrown over my thighs, her body tight against mine, our hands still touching, caressing, promising. "I can't stay," she said in a near whisper.

It was there and I thought my heart would stop, but it just kept beating away, and time kept moving forward.

"You have always been my hero, Bobby. When I was young and alone and found you, got to know you, I thought you were like a forest, a strong but secret place of calm where I could rest."

"A little rager like I was?" I asked with a mix of amusement and surprise.

"Like you *are*," she said, a smile in her voice. "Jake might have been the one who kept all us kids together, but you were the one that kept us safe. If anyone bothered us, you were there to make them stop. Don't you remember that?"

"I remember us," I told her. "I remember how we used to sneak out at night just to lay on that old wooden bridge, look up at the stars and talk about the future. How we'd run away together. How we'd be together forever."

I heard her sigh and felt bad for where I'd led the conversation.

She sighed again, and slipped her hand into mine, entwining her fingers with mine.

"You're still my strong calm forest. The place I come to rest. I guess you always will be. You just can't be with me all the time. I hope you can understand that. It's not who you are. It's who I am. Or rather, who I was, and who I want to be. I'm mixing this all up."

"There's a guy there, in Honduras." I said quietly.

"Yes, there's a guy. But that's not it. Shush. Let me talk. This is hard and I want to get it right." She squeezed my hand, and I said nothing.

"The Zoey you knew back then was a sad little girl. A scared person, a victim. She was your damsel in distress, and you were her knight, maybe not a white knight, but still . . ."

She kissed my shoulder. Then she paused a moment as if to get her thoughts straight. Finally, she said, "I needed a hero then. Someone strong to rescue me and show me that I could survive in this crazy, cruel world. Then I needed to become my own hero. It took a long time to get there. A whole lot of therapy. I won't tell you how much, but I think I've made it. I've turned a corner and I feel good about my life. I want to leave the past behind and move forward."

"With the guy in Honduras?" I hazarded a guess.

"Yes," she said, squeezing my hand. The guy in Honduras. His name is Robert. He's a doctor from a family of doctors from Colorado. It's one of their things, in their family, to volunteer their time when they're young, before they get married and settle down. So he volunteered with United Planet for six months. He was seeing these gang affected kids. Some had been shot, stabbed. There was one kid with a broken spine who didn't have a wheelchair. He had to drag himself on his elbows. The stories. God, they'd break your heart. After his six months was up, he couldn't leave.

He found some donors and started a clinic. Rented an old house at first and then they built a real clinic. It's changed things for so many of those kids. They get their basic needs met, maybe for the first time in their lives. There are two group homes, one for the boys and one for the girls. They even have a school now. That's where I come in. I've been taking online courses, getting my teaching certificate but I already help out. In fact, I'm actually teaching."

She said it with a sense of wonder that made me realize just how low her self-esteem had been. As if teaching had been a thing so far out of reach, she'd never imagined it for herself. Poor Zoey, so special and so unaware.

"I love it there," she continued. "It's a beautiful place if you can stand the heat. Of course, I spend as much time in the water as I can. Robert's teaching me to dive."

She had such a faraway look in her eyes it was as if she'd already gone.

"They see me differently," she explained. "All of them. But especially Robert. See, he doesn't know much about my past. He hasn't heard the ugly stories. When he looks at me, he sees a different me than you do. He doesn't see a victim or someone who needs rescue. He thinks I'm smart and competent. He doesn't see the scars I carry inside."

"You told me my scars were beautiful," I reminded her. "That you don't even see them."

"That's true, but the problem isn't that you see my scars, the problem is that when you look at me, I see them. Does that make sense?"

"No, not really. Nothing about you leaving makes sense. When we were kids, you said we'd always be together," I reminded her.

"But we didn't stay together, did we? We tried to escape through each other for a time, but it didn't work, so we kept leaving each other."

"I seem to remember you doing the leaving and me doing the waiting for you to come back."

"That's not true. You left for the Army. You took off on a road trip. You were gone for years."

"Because you left first."

"And you made it impossible to come back."

"Not true. You could have reached out. Jake always knew how to find me. You knew that." I wasn't going to make this easy for her. Not this time.

"I love Robert," she said as if that was the final word.

Her declaration didn't even make me pause. I said, "But does he love you? You know how beautiful you are. What if that's all he cares about. How do you know he doesn't just want you because you're exceptionally attractive, a former model, a trophy."

Zoey laughed, a short bark of a laugh. "Oh Bobby, you don't get it. Robert is smart and rich, charitable, and kind. He's also tall and gorgeous. If anything, he's the trophy. Besides, if he wanted a trophy wife, he could have one. But what he wants, crazy as it seems, is me. He told me once he was looking forward to us getting old and wrinkly so men would stop looking at me and he could have me to himself. Does that sound like someone who only cares about what a woman looks like?"

I had to admit it did not. I didn't want to like the guy, but he sounded like a decent human being. A man with a purpose who was helping people in a way I never could. If I were a better man, I'd probably tell her something about how great we had been and how I wished her a wonderful life with Robert. Instead, I said, "If you're so crazy about the guy why in hell are you in bed with me? Why the hell are you here?"

I tensed, anticipating that she'd strike out and slap or kick me. At the least I thought she'd cuss me out, tell me I was a jerk. She did none of those things.

Instead, she did something much worse. She slid her fingers across my forehead, down my temple to my jaw. Her fingertips were cool and soft against my heated skin.

“I’m so sorry,” she said. “I thought you understood. I’m here to say goodbye. Say goodbye to me, Bobby.”

CHAPTER TWENTY-NINE

Jake called on Tuesday morning and the jubilation in his voice made me want to stab him in the throat.

After our talk on Friday Zoey had stayed at my house. We'd eaten each meal together. Tidied up the house. Made runs for groceries and did other domestic things. We were playing house, and it was painful.

That morning she'd mentioned that maybe moving into the hotel for the rest of her stay might be the right thing to do. I hadn't said anything, just pulled her onto my lap and held her, felt her warm body against mine, breathed in her scent, tried to memorize the way she felt against me, warm and alive and present.

She had pressed her face against the side of my neck, and I felt warm tears as she sobbed quietly. A heartbreaking goodbye whose memory I knew would torture me far into the future.

I put down the phone and told Zoey that Jake had called, and it was time to go to his house. She nodded, then headed to the bathroom to wash her face, and dry her tears. Being strong and manly I merely scrubbed my hands across my face and went in search of the keys to Princess.

Jake was by himself when we arrived and as excited as a little boy on his birthday. He led us into the kitchen where we saw, in the center of the table, the half-sized padded manilla envelope.

"I checked the PO Box first thing this morning. Couldn't believe it showed up. I mean. I knew it was coming but to actually see it there. Do you want to open it?" He asked Zoey.

She smiled, somewhat indulgently I thought, like a mother to her child. An image of her as a mother brought a fresh wash of pain. She nodded and said, "Of course."

"Or should we call everyone?" he asked. "Get them all over here for this?"

I shook my head. I didn't want to prolong this. "They can come over later," I told him. "We'll have a celebration. You don't really want to wait, do you?"

"Hell no. Go for it, Zoey."

In one movement Zoey reached across the table, picked up the envelope, slid one short nail under the flap, and tore it open. Then she reached in, pinched the enclosed plexiglass between her fingers, and pulled it out. She laid it on the table, and we stared down in awe at Micheal Jorden's photo and autograph.

"That there, exclaimed Jake, is a two million dollar win for the good guys. We did it. We goddamn did it!"

He laughed and it was infectious. My sadness about Zoey leaving was still there but, for the moment, pushed back to the smallest corner of my conscious. We were happy, exuberant, and excited to share the good news. In the midst of high fiving and hugs Jake grabbed his phone and started making calls. Within an hour the so-called crew arrived to celebrate.

Once we'd gathered everyone in the living room Jake said, "Andy, Little Mikey and Heather were the only ones we told about the plan. We needed their help, but we figured if we left the rest of you out of the loop, you'd be better off if the cops got involved. No matter what they say, lie detectors are a bitch to pass."

"Sorry," I said, pointedly to Letitia, who looked like she was ready to chew nails. She gave me a crooked smile and a nod I took as forgiveness.

"It was Bobby's idea," Zoey said. She was sitting next to me on the couch and patted my leg when she said my name. "That day when I went to lunch with Hugh, he gave me a tour of his house. When I got back to Bobby's, I told him about everything I'd seen."

"She'd seen a lot," I told them. "From the way he had the new card on display in his office to the way his mail was stacked on a silver tray in the entry."

"Foyer," Zoey said, correcting me. "Rich people have foyers."

"Foyer," I said, nodding my agreement and smiling like a fool. I couldn't help it. Zoey sitting beside me, her hand resting on my leg was one of the good moments I'd file away.

"She told him about a lot of things," said Jake, but it was those two elements he put together, right?"

"Right," I said, "That's what gave me the idea. I didn't know what to do with it right away though.

Then Howie called. He told me two of our, uh friends, Lacey and Gracey, had been asked to go to the party. They work for Oliver."

"Sex workers?" Booker asked.

I nodded. "Yes. Hugh wanted pretty women there to impress the people he'd invited. Only they hate their boss, and I figured getting them to help screw over his brother would not be a problem."

"What kind of help?" asked Booker.

"Nothing dangerous. I just asked them to keep an eye on Rose and his men. Text me with who he had with him and where they were in the house."

"I see."

"Only they did more than that," said Zoey

"They sure did. You see, the plan changed. Instead of breaking into the building to steal from the collection I'd start a fire to destroy it. I knew that would set off all kinds of alarms, but Andy convinced me that by the time anyone had a chance to respond Jake and I would be long gone."

"But not too long gone," said Jake. "We wanted them to follow us."

"Why?" asked Nathan.

"To draw them away from the house and from Zoey. To give her a chance to do her magic."

"Ah, you're gonna make me blush," said Zoey. I wouldn't call it magic. It's more an old, rusty skill set."

"Now, don't be modest, Heather said. We'd never have dressed well or had pretty things when we were kids if it hadn't been for you. She got me this watch one time—"

"Hey, back to the story," said Zoey, blushing slightly. Her skills as a shoplifter were legendary, but not to be bragged about. "You see, Andy," she nodded toward him, and he beamed. "Andy was still looking into Hugh Rose and in his research, he saw an article about the party."

Andy said, "There was a picture of Hugh with the article. He was at his desk and the new card was right there in plain sight. I thought he probably locked it up at night, either in a safe in the house or out in the building where he kept the rest of his stuff. But for the party he'd have it out where he could show it off. It would just be sitting there." Andy wore a hungry smile that made him look like a starving man who had just been presented with a meal. "That was the key to the whole thing," I told them.

"And it went better than I expected," said Zoey, taking back the story. "My biggest problem was I couldn't get away from Hugh. He's one of those clingy people who always has to be touching you. His hand was always around my waist or on my back." She shuddered. "His guys moved around some, but one stayed in the kitchen most of the time, the other was just in the background wherever Hugh was. I couldn't ditch either of them.

"People kept arriving. I guess when Hugh figured there were enough, he led us upstairs to his office. He showed everyone the card and of course they all oohed and aahed. There were a lot of pretty people jammed in at that point. I noticed the second bodyguard had come upstairs, maybe so he wasn't the only one left out? Not sure why he was there but it seemed like the best time to let Bobby know he should go. I sent the text."

I laughed. "It said, go. So, I did."

Zoey smiled and continued, "An alarm went off somewhere in the house. Everyone tried to run for the stairs at the same time. I saw your friend, I think her name is Gracey, trip the bodyguard as he was going down the stairs. He tumbled and cracked his head on the hardwood floor. He was okay but it knocked him silly for a minute.

"That's why they were so slow getting to us," I said.

Zoey nodded. "That and because there were so many guests that Hugh and his other bodyguard had to practically climb over them. Of course, I stayed upstairs. Little ol' me afraid of being trampled." She batted her eyelashes at us, then continued.

"Everyone had left the office and were jammed in the landing area, trying to get down the stairs. Taking the fake card out of the clutch and switching it for the real one was easier than lying." Zoey smiled a very Zoey smile.

Heather said, "The clutch has a concealed section. It's supposed to conceal a gun but hey, whatever you need to hide." Mikey, who was sitting beside her, bent and kissed her nose. She giggled and smacked his chest affectionately.

Zoey said, "The other thing in the clutch was a manilla envelope, one of those half size ones. I put the real card inside it, sealed it, and held it alongside the clutch. Then I followed the crowd downstairs. Everyone was milling around the entryway—"

"Foyer," I said, correcting her.

She smiled at me, shook her head and said, "Anyway, I let the crowd move me toward the door. Some people had gone outside to see what the fuss was all about, including Hugh. When I reached the table by the door, I slipped the envelope into the outgoing mail stacked on the tray. After that I poked my nose out for a moment.

"People were noticing the building was on fire by then. Flames filled every window. Hugh was yelling. The alarm was deafening but I could hear sirens in the distance. Someone had called the fire department. Maybe Hugh. Maybe a neighbor.

"The trucks arrived. It was total chaos. People started to leave and that caused a traffic jam. Cops showed up and they managed to unsnarl the traffic and let the firetrucks do their thing."

"That must have been nuts," said Nathan

"Totally nuts," Zoey agreed. "Hugh finally came in and shut off the alarm. I caught a ride with one of the departing guests. Had them drop me at my hotel. The end."

There was a hush of silence when she was done, then everyone started to talk at once. I heard Booker ask, "You sure we can get that much for it?"

"My uncle is handling it," I heard Andy respond. For ten precent he said he'd come out of retirement for a few hours. Ten percent of two million. That's a pretty good score."

The room went silent again.

"How are we going to divide that much money?" Zoey, asked. I was beginning to realize that she was probably the most pragmatic of us.

"I've been giving that some thought," said Jake. "If we do get the expected two million and pay the fence his half and Andy's uncle his ten percent.

"Ten percent of the full two," said Andy. The fence won't share cost."

Jake nodded. "Yeah, so you said. So that leaves us eight hundred thousand. Letitia lost one hundred thousand. I say we make her whole. Does everyone agree?"

Everyone did.

"And I said I'd pay Bobby fifty percent as a finder's fee, said Letitia."

"Yeah, but I think it should come from the big pot, not out of your money."

"But that's—" Letitia tried to say something but was cut off by Jake.

"Everyone agree?"

Everyone did.

"Nathan, you owe fifty thousand. We're going to give you that to pay yourself out of debt."

"Thank you," Booker and Nathan said in unison.

"That leaves six hundred thousand," said Heather.

We all looked at her.

"Don't look so surprised. I'm slow, not stupid." Then she laughed, and we laughed with her.

"Okay," said Jake. Heather's right. That leaves six-hundred thousand that we damn sure better not spend right away. If you trust me, I'd like to hold onto it awhile and then later divide it equally between everyone here, except for Nathan, who got us into this and shouldn't get a reward for it. You all good with that?" he asked.

Nathan didn't say a word. He just nodded. He really was learning.

"We can't put the money in a savings account at the bank. That would create a paper trail, but I can lock it up in a safe deposit box. I'm thinking it should sit for at least nine months, like a fetus that needs time to grow.

"That's a real big baby," said Leticia. She shot a glance at Booker. He had, after all, ripped her off. But she didn't say anything about the distribution Jake proposed.

Jake nodded, suddenly serious. "I'll take care of it I promise and get it to you in cash. I put it into a calculator earlier and it comes to sixty-six thousand six hundred and a bunch of sixes each."

"The number of the beast," I said under my breath. It seemed fitting. Some of the lyrics to Iron Maiden's "Hallowed Be They Name," ran through my mind. *The sands of time for me are running low*. I put my hand on top of Zoeys, pinning it there.

"It *is* a big baby, but I bet we can find good ways to spend it," Jake was saying to Heather. "You and Mikey can consider it a wedding present and go on a killer delayed honeymoon. Letitia and Tilly, I'm sure you can find a use for some money with that new farm. Booker, you can travel or help Nathan with college, or whatever the hell you want. Andy, you can start on a new career, get some training, or at least move into your own place when you're ready. Bobby, well hell, what Bobby will spend it on is anyone's guess.

"As for me, I'm putting mine in the foster family fund. It's a savings account I draw on to help the kids who spent time with us at the Sparrows. Sometimes I use it for other foster kids I hear about who need something. You know most of us don't have real family to help us, so we have to help each other. Oh, and Bobby said we should give some to Gracey and Lacey, so I'll take care of that."

While Jake was talking about how he'd unselfishly use his cut I considered how I'd use mine. If my math was right, I'd walk away with a bundle. For starters, I'd be able to pay Jake back, start paying rent, and feel a lot less like a charity case. I should have been elated.

Instead, all I could focus on was how every moment was bringing me closer to Zoey leaving.

As if my thinking of her had brought her to Jake's mind he said, "Zoey, you told me about the kids you work with in Honduras. I got a feeling I know where your money is going."

"Maybe. Even probably. But it sounds like I'll have to wait awhile. In the meanwhile, could I take everyone out for waffles? I'm starving."

After less than a minute of debate, it turned out she could.

CHAPTER THIRTY

Two days later Jake and I stood at a window in the airport at PDX and watched Zoey's plane slip away into an achingly blue sky. The clear sky seemed wrong. It should have been cloudy and raining.

"You okay?" Jake asked.

"Nope."

"Didn't think so. You gonna be okay?"

I shrugged.

"Give it time."

I nodded.

"You said you were going to start looking for a job after this got dealt with."

"Uh huh," I said, turning from the window and trudging down the long hallway toward the exit. Jake walked along beside me.

"The thing is. You remember Dale Preston?" he asked.

I had to think about it a moment. Then the image came to me, a pale boy with a freckled face and red hair.

"Dale. He stayed with us about six or seven months, right?"

"Yeah, he was the one set his room on fire."

"Sure, I remember him. Hard to forget. What about him?"

"Well, he's in trouble. Got arrested but he swears he was set up. That he didn't do it."

"Do what?"

"Arson."

"Seriously?"

"I know. But he told me he turned his life around, started a successful business, was running for local office. He was really making a name for himself. Now someone has taken that away from him. He swears he didn't start the fire and I believe him."

"You would."

"You will too once you talk to him. I think you could help him."

"Help him?"

"Yeah, help him recover his good name, like you helped Letitia recover what was taken from her. Take it and give it back."

I stared at him not disguising my disbelief.

He tugged at his beard. "Oh, I see. You thought Letitia was a one off. He smiled, a Jake about to dive headlong into trouble smile, and said, "Nah, Letitia was just the first. Don't you get it, you have a new purpose my friend, you're not Bobby Fucking Poe anymore. Nope, now you're the Repoe Man. Get it, Re. Poe."

"You're such an asshole," I told him.

"I know," he said, "I missed you too."

ABOUT THE AUTHOR

Pamela Cowan is a Pacific Northwest author best known for her contemporary mystery and suspense thrillers. She lives in Oregon where she spends her time writing, gardening, and hiking. She has two grown children, a wonderful husband, and a dog determined to end the tyranny of UPS, USPS, and FedEx, drivers. To date, she has not succeeded.

If you enjoyed this novel, please leave a review on Amazon or Goodreads. Reviews are invaluable to both readers and authors. It's how we find each other.

Learn more about Pamela's novels and short fiction at her website, pamelacowan.com where you can sign up for her newsletter and learn about new releases, events, and more.

www.ingramcontent.com/pod-product-compliance
Lightning Source LLC
Chambersburg PA
CBHW072116250626
47159CB00007B/2473
* 9 7 8 1 9 5 7 6 3 8 9 6 6 *